BLACK COUNTRY
STORIES
&
SKETCHES

GREG STOKES

First Published By THE KATES HILL PRESS
126 Watsons Green Road, Dudley, DY2 7LG

Copyright © Greg Stokes February 1993.

ISBN: 0 9520317 0 1

British Library CIP Data:
A catalogue record for this book is available
from the British Library

Printed By THAMESLINK, Windsor, Berkshire.

Cover Design By Sue Graham.

BLACK COUNTRY STORIES & SKETCHES

FOR:

MOM, CAROL,

LOUISE & LUCY

Many people have contributed to these stories, often without knowing it. In particular, my thanks to my sister, Jill Bowen (The Inheritance); Steve Harding (The Dunkirk Spirit, On Leave, Tommy Stone's Send Off); the late Jim Jones (On Leave); Brenda Cooper (Street Scene); Chris Workman (The Effrontery, Christmas Card To Lev); my uncle, Des Stokes (Baldwin's Monument); my father, the late Doug Stokes (Tim The Tatter); my maternal grandmother, the late Matilda Baxter (Grandma's Apparition); Lance Whitehouse (Shafted); and my father's cousin, Jack Stokes (The Blue Teapot).

THE INHERITANCE

1) The Notification

Derek Timms knew of many arguments about where the Black Country was. There were probably thousands of definitions, some of them vastly different. They all had one common feature however; the Black Country does not include any of Birmingham.

That made it interesting for Derek when he started work in Birmingham. His uncle Jack had warned him that Brummies tended to extend their boundaries to encompass places they wouldn't know how to get to. Jack reckoned that this was because Birmingham city centre was nowhere near the centre of the city of Birmingham. Brummies from the city's vast east side didn't seem to be able to grasp that Brum finishes and the Black Country starts past Handsworth. Jack also warned Derek that he would receive many a ribbing about his accent which would stick out like a sore thumb over there contrary to a popular belief outside the midlands that they sounded the same.

Derek Timms had been at Vulcan Components in Adderley Park for about nine months. He sat at his desk contemplating.

Monday. His whole life seemed to be Sunday nights and Monday mornings. You spend all the week looking forward to the weekend then no sooner than the weekend arrives, there it is; Sunday night. Monday morning eve. He wondered how many times that thought had crossed his mind and yet here it was again, Monday morning. Maybe he should start thinking of Tuesday as Monday morning Boxing Day to continue his analogy of that part of the week with Christmas. He liked Boxing Day a lot better than Christmas Day; all the pubs were open for a start and there was a full football programme. Under that system he would be able to look upon Tuesday as a good day. The trouble was that he liked Christmas Eve but he didn't like Sunday night so the analogy broke down there.

He chewed this problem over as he gazed through the office window at the spring sky. It was early April and starting to warm up a bit. Derek started to think of decades. It was the first spring of the new decade. the winter hadn't been nearly as harsh this year. Throughout the early months of 1979 the weather had been appalling. The sporting calendar had taken a hell of a beating to testify to it. 1980 seemed to be much better year, some of the earlier blossoms were starting to show through and the pitch at Molineux was looking a bit greener, Derek thought. But no matter what time of the year it was, it was always Monday morning. He recalled the

Justin Hayward song from a few years before called *Forever Autumn* and wondered when someone would write one entitled *Forever Monday*.

On the other side of the office Jim Roberts sat at his desk. Jim had not endeared himself to Derek from the moment they first met. When asked whence he hailed, Derek's reply "Tipton." elicited the opinion that it was not the nicest part of the city. Derek's reply that he was not aware that it was part of the "city" fell on deaf ears. If things were bad culturally, politically they were far worse; Jim was the company union basher.

The phone on Jim's desk rang. He put down his coffee and answered it.

"It's for you Timms," he said with a frown.

Derek got up and walked across to take the call. Jim handed him the receiver saying "You're not supposed to have people phone you at work you know."

Derek didn't reply but gave him instead a dirty look, about force four on his truculence scale of one to ten. It was the first incoming call he had had since starting there.

"Hello."

"Hello. Derek?" said the voice at the other end of the line which was not immediately recognisable to him.

"Yes, speaking."

"Ar, good, yoe sound different on the phone. It's yer uncle Frank here...."

"Oh. Frank. I day [didn't] recognise ya. How bin [are] ya?"

Derek sat down on Jim's desk. Frank was Jack's brother. In a split second the thought crossed Derek's mind, 'uncle Jack is dead.'

"Your uncle Jack is dead." Frank confirmed. There was a silence while the terrible news hovered before the dialogue, the pattern of which seemed time honoured, continued. It was on Frank to say how and where.

"Heart attack, sudden. Happened this morning in Dudley market place."

"How's aunt Flo tekin it?"

"It's knocked her about a bit. Her seems alright but it ay sunk in yet, for none on we."

It was true that it hadn't sunk in and asking how someone felt was a bit futile because the feeling is usually one of numbness when one first hears of the death of a loved one. The rest of existence shuts off and one does not "feel" anything. The questions were all part of a time honoured ritual however so it had to be continued.

"How'd it happen?"

"They was going shopping up Dudley, went early. They got off the bus at Fisher Street and walked up to the Market Place. On his way up he said how well he felt. Outside Woolworths he fainted, or that's what it looked

6

like. Luckily a policeman come up and sid [saw] as he'd had a heart attack and got that special ambulance on his radio."

"The mobile cardiac unit."

"Ar, that's it. They'd got to him on time and they rushed him to Burton Road and took him to the intensive care. On'y bin there five minutes and he had another one, a massive one. They couldn't save him that time. Five to ten it was. They did everything they could mate."

It was now up to Derek to ask what was becoming more and more important because the answer was becoming less and less yes.

"Was anybody with him at the last."

"Ar, yer aunt Flo was there. They took her in the ambulance as well."

In olden days people died in the presence of their family. "Was anybody there?" would not have been part of the ritual; someone was always there. Nowadays we are all doomed to shuttle off this mortal coil in the company of strangers, a very lonely and tragic moment. To have someone there at the last is a great comfort all round. Derek felt the blow softened in the knowledge that his beloved uncle Jack hadn't departed in loneliness.

"He wor [wasn't]on his own mate. Thank God."

"Did he know much, did he say anything?"

"I don't think he knew a lot about it at the end so he cor [can't] have suffered a lot. That's a God send." Frank gave a little laugh before he continued. "When they got him into the hospital he said 'I hope it doe [doesn't]mean I miss me Thursday pint with our Derek'. Jack to the last."

Jack to the last. That too was a comforting thought to Derek.

"He thought a lot of you yer know Derek?"

"Ar Frank. Me too." Derek replied softly. "Me too." There was a silence for a few seconds then it was on Derek to round off the ritual.

"Is there anything I can do?"

"Well not unless you want a lot of upset folk around you. No mate, leave it to me. I shall see you tonight." Frank said almost clinically. He was upset alright but for now, he knew he had to cope.

"Ar, tonight. See you Frank....And thanks." Derek put the receiver down slowly. He shuffled round off the desk and stood up. He felt alright but he had gone quite pale. The rest of the office was in silence and they were all looking at him. They overheard enough of the tell-tale ritual to have gathered what was wrong.

Paul Danks had welcomed Derek's arrival at the firm. He too was a Black Country man working "abroad". He broke the silence. "Bad news?"

"Uncle Jack."

"I'm sorry mate." Paul said clasping him by the shoulder. "Here, sit down."

Jim opened the bottom drawer of his desk and pulled out a half bottle of brandy, untapped, and a glass. He poured out a liberal amount and brought it over to Derek.

"Here, drink this. I've been saving it for emergencies."

Derek looked up and declined the offer with shake of his head.

"Drink it." Jim insisted. "It'll do you good."

"Drink it down chap." Paul agreed. "You might not think it but you are in a state of shcck."

Derek took the glass and knocked back a mouthful. The heat of the spirit bit into his senses.

"Put the kettle on again and make some more coffee." Jim said, taking charge of the situation.

Derek took another mouthful of brandy and reality seemed to return.

Just then the boss came in but Jim told him the score. Derek's news threw him. He left without saying what he had come for.

Derek had gone full spectrum from the numbness following the news in which his consciousness was diffuse, through the in-tune-body-and-soul reality brought on by the shock of the spirit, to the constricted consciousness which was a result of the knowledge that everyone was looking at him. He sat at his own desk looking straight ahead, but he perceived things as though his eyes were at the end of a tunnel. He heard himself speaking.

"Know what the last thing he said was?" He didn't perceive a reply or any acknowledgement that he had spoken, which is not to say that he had not been given one. He heard himself continue. "He said 'I hope it doe mean as I miss me Thursday pint with Derek.'" He heard himself laugh, the laugh of respect of certainty. "I'll be there. Jack'll be there too." He perceived the tunnel to his eyes getting shorter as his conscious expanded and he was back in the office, his senses back where they should be in relation to it. He saw the mug of coffee in front of him.

Paul ran him back to Tipton.

2) Condolences

Derek's flat seemed stark, empty, almost unlived in despite the ever-present bachelor mess. It was getting on for twelve. He would go for a walk, a long walk, maybe along the canals. But he would get some dinner first from the chip shop round the corner. Then he would end up in *The George and Dragon* in Princes End. Some of Jack's oldest mates called in there for a pint at dinner time. They would have to be told the sad news. He would tell them; someone had to. In the warm April sunshine he slowly made his way down towards Princes End and he had that feeling one only gets in spring, as feeling of optimism and newness as the earth has been reborn. That feeling made it all the more difficult for it to sink in that uncle Jack was no longer on this earth.

The lunchtime trade in *The George and Dragon* couldn't be described as brisk. Besides, there is no lunchtime in most of the Black Country; there is breakfast, dinner, and tea. Lunch was for posh folks and no one of that ilk frequented *The George* at any rate. There were at most a dozen people in. A few had been laid off recently, a few were on short time and didn't go in until Wednesday, a few were on dinner break from work. One was actually from that mysterious band "half of 'em who don't want any work". He hadn't done a tap for fifteen years and hadn't any plans on doing a tap in the next fifteen either but he, and his kind, didn't constitute 50% of the jobless in the pub or anywhere else. The remaining half dozen or so were pensioners; Jack's mates.

The gaffer recognised Derek and asked him what he was doing in there of a dinner time. He sensed bad news when he read the look on Derek's face. When his fears were confirmed a few seconds later he relieved Derek of the job of informing the others. There was no reverence in the way he shouted the news across the room to the others who were sat around a table. Neither was there any disrespect in it for in a bar that is the way things are announced. The news was greeted with a sense of amazement for it was a surprise to everyone that such a spritely chap as Jack should have passed on. Such comments as "I on'y sid [saw] him last wik [week]" and "He was right as ninepence th'other day" were heard but there was no outward sign of sorrow. There never is when a bar loses one of its number. The game had to go on; there were a few shillings riding on the 2 o'clock race, the Wolves and the Albion would be playing on Saturday and only seven holes needed to be pegged for the game. The dominoes rattled on. The gaffer would have no money from Derek for his pint and one by one, in their own time, Jack's mates came up to offer their condolences. And in their own time they would have their moments of grief to come to terms with what had happened. Derek didn't know when the funeral was yet, he would let them know. He left declining the gaffers offer of another pint. The gaffer thought as he watched him go, he would have to organise a collection for the widow.

3) The Committal

The cortége made its way down slowly down the Newton Road. Tipton was now part of Sandwell so it was the road to Sandwell crematorium which was to be Jack's last journey. Newton Road was an ancient highway but is now a dual carriageway connecting West Bromwich with Perry Barr.

It runs across the green strip of Sandwell Valley which is the only recognisable physical separation between the Black Country and Birmingham. Cars zoomed past as the convoy approached the crem at the bottom of the valley. Over to the right, on top of the hill, the sun glinted on the floodlights at the Hawthorns. The whole valley was positively verdant.

A fairly large crowd was waiting outside the crem; distant family, close friends, life-long acquaintances, ex work-mates, the bar room of *The George*. Derek had said that it would have to be all ticket. He retained his composure up to that point, so too till the service began. At other cremations he had been to he had tried to think of the Billy Connolly spiel where a bloke pokes his head through the curtains at the committal and asks if anyone has got a match. The loss was too great at this one. His composure dissolved as the congregation sang 'Abide With Me'. Why do they sing that at Cup Finals he thought, trying to regain control. But it was to no avail as his tears flowed. It was nothing to be ashamed of however. He looked across at the bereaved brother, Frank, who raised a smile from beneath his tears for his nephew. Derek battled in vain to control his emotions. He had wanted to say goodbye with a degree of decorum, he had wanted for the first time in his life to stand to attention and to salute his uncle Jack for he was one of the few people he had met worthy of it. The emotions won in the end, easily. There was nothing undignified about it, it was the natural releasing of the stress the bereavement had caused. The service ended and the vicar shook hands with everyone on the way out. A gentle breeze wafted towards the Albion ground. Frank looked up and noticed the direction of the wind. He smiled, Jack would be happy up there.

The rest of the congregation followed the cortége back to Princes End. The neighbours were out in the street to watch the family return. A posse of them had been getting things ready while the family were away; cutting sandwiches and brewing gallons of tea. The gaffer from *The George* had donated a barrel of mild to the proceedings. He had known Jack since childhood and his dad and Jack's dad had been big mates also.

The send off went as all working class send offs with a polarisation between those with their feet on the ground and those with pretensions to being up market. Derek got on well with his immediate family and Jack's mates but a number of people he rarely saw were taking great interest in him having a degree. "What degree have you got?" "Which college did you go to? London. Ooh, that's good isn't it? Such and suches son only went to Loughborough. That isn't a real university is it?" "What job do you do? Is it high up? Are the prospects good? Does it pay well?" "When are you getting married? I'll bet he's got someone hidden away somewhere." Derek stayed out of misplaced politeness. Frank rescued him saying that the barrel needed tapping. When he got through, the barrel had already been tapped but he stayed put. With the real people he thought. The "What degree have you got" crew were real too in that they existed but they had an air of unreality about them to Derek when he put them alongside Jack's mates. Did they really think that having a degree mattered, that Loughborough wasn't a real university. He shuddered at the thought of the class to which he was now a part but consoled himself that he was in the good company of the sort of people which make an area what it is. The talk turned to football. The Wolves and Albion followers vied for supremacy with tales of former greatness. After a few pints Frank came over to Derek and said "Your aunt Flo wants to see you for a couple of minutes. I think you're going to be coming into some money young man."

4) The Inheritance

Frank led the way to aunty Flo who was in the main bedroom though it wasn't that Derek was unaware of the route. She was seated with her back to the window, her hands clasped together in her lap. Her posture was erect and displayed dignity, the dignity with which she had conducted herself throughout the day. Frank closed the door behind him shutting the three of them off in a sort of familial inner sanctum. Aunty Flo spoke slowly but firmly giving her dialect pronunciation the crispness that elocution lessons give users of Oxon English.

"After we lost Ronald, your uncle Jack came into some money. I was too old to have any more kids and Franks two were growed up so he put it away for you to have when you got wed. We day tell you about it afore in case some fast ooman got her hooks in when you was still young."

Derek smiled at that comment. She continued. "Jack never lived to see you get wed as he wanted to because he looked upon you as he would his own. That was the last big thing for Jack, to see your wedding, but it wor [wasn't] to be. So, now Jack's gone the money's your'n."

"But surely the money should be left for you, or for Frank."

Flo and Frank smiled at each other as Jack had said that Derek would say that if he was to go first. Flo resumed. "I've got enough put by to last me. What with me pension and all, and Frank's alright. No, this money was put by special in a trust fund. Its probably worth quite a bit now as he'd been adding to it over the years."

Frank added his support to the statement. Derek shook his head.

"No, I'm sorry, I couldn't tek [take] any money. It should go to you two. Times are getting hard again."

Flo wasn't going to be put off by Derek's remonstrations.

"That money is for you, it had been put aside specially. I've been looked after in the will and the house is our own so I'll be alright."

Derek looked to Frank hoping for support which wasn't forthcoming.

"Me and the wife have got enough put by. Besides, our own kids look after us."

Flo took up the argument again. "Listen Derek, you'll have that money. Its what Jack wanted. As you say, times are getting hard. It is getting like the 'thirties again with so many people out of work." She smiled as she had begun to reminisce. "You are just like Jack when he was young. He was an idealist, wanted to change the world. He was in the Communist Party when he was eighteen, 1930 that was. They used to have meetings in the Shakespeare up Dudley High Street. That pub's gone now of course. You didn't know that did you?"

"I never knew he was in the party, he never said."

"No, he never told you that because you took after him so much. He didn't want you to go and join one of these left wing groups, not until you knew your own mind at any rate. He soon left when he found out that not many of them shared his ideals. They were steeped in party dogma. The ends justified the means was the excuse though a lot of them had lost sight of the ends. It was just a game of means. Then there was the depression and the unions couldn't stop jobs being lost or create new ones. After that there was the war and Jack's generation were called up like his father's in the one before. He already knew by then though that a working man couldn't change the world by himself. All that he can do is try to look after those closest to him, family and friends, as best he can without hurting anybody else in the process. That's how Jack lived his life out after the war, he'd stopped wanting to change the world, he just helped those around him as best he could. That didn't make him any less of an idealist. He still dreamt of a better world on the horizon." She paused in happy memory of her departed husband. "You take the money Derek, having some money by you won't make you any less of an idealist either. It may help you through a rough patch, you could find yourself out of work next week. As I've said, its getting like the 'thirties again with all the blokes getting thrown out of work. Its not decent for a man to be out of work, he loses all his self respect. I know we bay [aren't] going hungry this time so maybe we have got a better world in some ways. But we have got just as much lost pride, so you swallow your pride a bit Derek because you might be needing that money. Besides its what Jack wanted."

Derek didn't speak at first, he just nodded. He too had wanted to change the world, still did to a certain extent. But of late he had begun to feel powerless to stop the recession which had been hitting his homeland so hard. He thought for a while and at length said simply "Yes. thankyou very much," and walked out.

Frank and Flo exchanged smiles. Jack wasn't dead, he had just left the room. Frank followed him not long after. Flo wished to be alone, she had seen enough people for one day.

Later in the day news came through that Vulcan Components was going onto a 3 day week. It was more sad news on a sad day. It would not be long before Derek had cause to use his inheritance.

THE DUNKIRK SPIRIT

Another Friday morning in the accounts office. Friday morning was the time for what had turned into the weekly joke of guessing when the management would call them to the office for the last rites. One can judge the morale of a place by its standing jokes. What time was indeed the question at Charles Newcombes (Engineering). The offices overlooked Netherton Church on its hill as the factory had been built not far from the Dudley canal. The whole area was one of works great and small which had grown along the banks of the canal which had been the motorway of the early industrial revolution. In the distance was Round Oak, the mightiest works of all; once the flagship of Lord Dudley's mineral empire, now part of British Steel. Rumours were rife Round Oak was closing. What would happen to Brierley Hill then? Newcombes was closer to Woodside in Dudley. Most of the workforce were from the local estates.....

Diane had already lost the bet, she always said ten. Johnny Hyde said ten thirty this week. Peter Snow said it would be eleven. At ten twenty the phone on Ralph Donaldson's desk rang. The kettle on the side table was beginning to boil and the half empty coffee jar waited for some more of its contents to be spooned into the cups. Ralph put the receiver down having just answered the call with a rather servile affirmative. "Hyde, Snow," he announced, "and you Miss Metcalfe. Mr Dodds wants to see you all in his office."

The three exchanged *this could be it* looks.

"Now." Ralph added at length as a thin smile began to curl his lips. Maybe this was it, his long awaited promotion. The three trooped out as the kettle lid began to rattle under the pressure of the steam.

It was it. A number of men from the works were outside the office awaiting their turn for the last rites. Everyone was standing there as though six of the best were about to be administered by a headmaster who had just discovered some widespread misdemeanour. The first one was still in however so it hadn't actually been confirmed yet.

A thin young man still in his teens emerged from the office. He was totally within himself. A third question to the effect: was it the end? from anxious workmates finally got through and received a nod to the affirmative. Silence followed the confirmation and realisation of fate diffused through the ranks. Where there is life there is hope. The life and the hope had just been dashed. They had come to work as normal and were to go home jobless.

Johnny looked about him and noticed that he and Peter were probably the oldest there and reckoned they must be telling the young ones first. He was correct. Dodds was carrying out the executions on a last in first out basis, even if the exits were only to differ by a few hours whereas the entrances differed by up to forty years. It could all have been done by letters but Dodds regarded that as cold blooded. He thought that a face to face approach would be better, and more polite, for something as important as telling a person they were out of work.

The last of the young factory workers had been dealt with so now it was the turn of the young staff workers to be told the news, though by now it was hardly news. The sales office staff answered their call and their worst suspicions were confirmed by the waiting queue. Diane was first in for accounts and Johnny next. Peter took his turn after Johnny, who, sombre-faced and silent, gave him a single nod on leaving the office. Peter stiffened his posture and with an almost military gait strode into Dodds' office. He had been the union rep for the staff side for some four years and would meet his fate without a blindfold.

In the office Dodds was seated behind his desk on his leather chair - which was slightly higher than the more basic chair on the other side, giving him a psychological advantage.

"Good morning Peter. Take a seat."

Peter sat down and returned the compliment, aware though that it was no good morning for him or any of the other occupants of that seat throughout the day.

"I expect you know what is happening, that was inevitable once I'd seen the first few, but I wanted to see everyone personally. I'm seeing the people who haven't been with the company too long first, then people who have been here for ten years and so on. The longest serving members of staff will be seen by the senior executive. Mr Donaldson for example, he's been with us for thirty years now." Dodds paused before starting his official message.

"The board now feels that the company is no longer a viable proposition and has therefore decided that the only course of action is to cease operations immediately. All the workforce are to be made redundant. So it is my unpleasant duty to say to you, I'm sorry, but it is the end of the line. This is where we all get off Peter, me included."

Dodds sank back in his chair expecting a tirade of abuse from the union man. Peter looked straight at Dodds, as he had done throughout his speech, and said, "Do you realise, this is the first time I've been to see you that you've been here on time."

Dodds allowed himself a short laugh. Peter was at the wrong end of the firing squad to go out with guns blazing.

"Yes," he said at length, "a deliberate tactic of mine I must admit. And it used to work sometimes."

"Sometimes." Peter conceded.

"You've been with us for what? Eight years now isn't it?"

Peter nodded. He had joined Newcombes straight from school.

"And you've been the union rep for four years. You've served your members well, I'll say that for you. And on the work side you've saved this company no small amount of money with your ideas. Having done those eight years with us you are entitled to some redundancy payment. Mr Donaldson and Mrs Cowley will be staying on an extra week to organise the redundancy cheques and what have you. You can call in early next week for it, or we can post it on."

"Post it." Peter snapped. He wouldn't want to see the place again once 'hanging day' was over.

"The only thing that remains is for me to wish you the very best of luck for the future and don't hesitate to use me as a reference if needs be. Your union activities won't be used against you."

Dodds rose and offered Peter his hand across the desk. Peter shook it firmly.

"Goodbye then." Dodds said, almost sadly. "All the best."

"Yes, all the best." Peter replied with no emotion in his voice. He made his exit in the same manner in which he made his entrance.

"Could you send in the first one from sales." The now seated Dodds said clinically.

Outside in the corridor Johnny and Diane had waited so that they could make their final journey to accounts as a team.

"Did you tell him what for?" Diane asked.

"Not a lot of point. He'll be out of work too. Mind you, I bet it'll be easier for him to find a job."

"Not necessarily." Diane replied.

Back in the office the kettle was still warm and three mugs remained on the tray waiting to be filled. Johnny went over to do the honours. Ralph didn't know the score and Peter knew that Ralph didn't know the score. There had been much animosity between the two over the years, Ralph was a confirmed union basher. It would only take one remark to spark Peter off.

Ralph watched them, looking extremely smug. Peter observed his superciliousness with growing disdain. His behaviour in Dodds office had been exemplary but his anger had still been there, a wrath that would have to be vented somewhere before very long, preferably on someone like Ralph. Keep it up Ralph, Peter thought.

Now Ralph had been brought up not to kick a man when he is down. His whole generation had, and yet, like many of his own and succeeding generations, he couldn't resist it when he got the chance. And for Ralph it would be especially difficult as it was one of those unionites, those commies, who was down.

"That's you then is it?" Ralph asked with undisguised spite.

"This is me Ralph, yes. Was that a physical or a philosophical observation?" Peter spat back, mocking Ralph's intelligence.

"That's you out of a job then is it?" Ralph corrected himself.

"Yes that's me out of a job Ralph. Happy?" Peter replied, drawing Ralph towards an outrageous comment.

"Yes it does. This country would be far better off if it sent all you bloody commies back to Russia where you belong." Ralph answered with venom.

"Back to Russia! Moron! Union: commie; commie: Russia; union: Russia. That's how your mind works isn't it. Do you know they don't allow free trade unions in Russia..."

Ralph was not really listening. Peter moved in for the kill.

"I suppose you think that with one less commie around this company will function a lot more smoothly."

"Yes I do!" Ralph snapped back. "Any concern is going to be better off without the likes of you. You don't seem to realise that you are bringing this country to its knees and we are not going to put up with it."

Peter was now ready to exact revenge for what he saw as Ralph's stupid ill-considered remarks over the years. He changed his tone from one of anger to one of complete calm.

"Its not just me they've got rid of though. There's Diane and Johnny too, and that's just for starters."

"I know they have to leave too but...."

"I'll tell you who else as well. I'll tell you just exactly who else is going as well and then we'll see how long that stupid smile stays on that stupid face of yours."

Peter moved across to deliver his last sentence right to Ralph's face.

Johnny intervened. "Hold up," he whispered to him, "it'll be bad enough when it does come. He's got nothing after this. We're young, we'll work again. He won't." That had the effect of stopping Peter momentarily for reflection but he turned to continue his quest. Johnny again intervened adding "He can't help it if he's a moron. Let him have his couple of hours."

Peter gave Ralph a long contemptuous look then returned to his desk to clear out his possessions.

Ralph watched him. He was enjoying his couple of hours for he didn't know that was all he had got.

"We are all going down the pub at dinner." Johnny announced to Ralph and Moira Cowley. "Care to join us for a farewell drink?"

Moira felt she had put up with a lot from Peter and Johnny over the years. She too would have a go. "You are just like that lot over in the factory, all you care about is drink. You go ahead, be lower class, piss all your money up a wall."

To Johnny, an inverted snob, the words were a compliment. He kissed Mrs Cowley on the cheek. Before her discomfiture could manifest Peter shouted over. "Put her down chap, don't know where she's been. There's no time any road, they'm open."

They trooped off to the pub leaving Ralph and Moira to their fate. The pub was already crowded by the time they got there and the mood was one of joviality. Newcombes may have become defunct but the workforce would go out with a bang.

The young men from the factory were playing darts. Theirs was a feeling, for the time being at any rate, of school holidays starting early. For those who were married the harsh realities would soon bite home.

There was no space to get to the bar as those with ten to twenty years service had come down mob-handed. These were the people who would do best out of it, if such a thing could be said. The younger people would pick up little or no redundancy money, not having put enough time in. On top of this, since jobs in their field would become more scarce, the jobs that were open would ask for experience and again they hadn't put enough time in to be considered. The middle length of service staff would pick up a reasonable amount of redundancy money and would have enough work left in them and the experience to be considered for the jobs which became available. No one's mind however was on such considerations. Having a bit of a session was the order of the day.

Over at the factory the senior executive had arrived. The oldest serving employees of Newcombes were to be told at noon.

The landlord called his wife through to help clear the early onslaught. He would have to make hay while the sun shone. A large proportion of his trade was from Newcombes at dinner time and early evenings. Being a tenancy, this was another related trade that would probably go under as part of the knock-on effect of recession.

The women from packing arrived and the mood changed to one of blatant innuendo. The juke box was fed and dancing music blared out, the party was in full swing. The beer flowed; the people laughed, the people danced, the people even sang when they knew the words, the people lived; if but for the moment.

The last of the last rites having been administered, the senior executive left the factory shrouded in the same obscurity with which he arrived. Even the older members of staff had doubted the existence of 'the old man' until that day. The veterans went to the pub. It was their party as much as anyone's.

Ralph and Moira were among the last to enter. They had been carried there by the tide of peer group pressure. Ralph was wearing a brave face but Moira had obviously been crying. One of the women from packing took Moira under her wing. Moira recoiled. Her repugnance of anything proletarian was all but complete. The packing lady was not to be put off. They were all in the same boat now and all the airs and graces in the world wouldn't put anyone in a different one. Now was the time for a party, she didn't know why, it just was. And everyone was to enjoy themselves; including Moira.

For two hours the party swung. Even Moira, her resolve steeled by a number of gins and the knowledge that it would only be for a while, got up to dance.

By two o'clock one or two started to trickle away, their goodbyes having been said. The crocodile tears were beginning to flow, just like last day at school when the seconds tick away and soon that assembly of people united in one establishment will be forever no more. There were the usual promises of keeping in touch, but it is a promise seldom kept.

Ralph was ready to leave. He had kept out of Johnny and Peter's way. Even he knew that they now had just cause to mock. That mocking would be too much to bear as he still felt himself to be right. Johnny noticed that he was about to go and went over to him.

"All the best Ralph. Mind how ya goo," he said, offering his hand.

Ralph shook it, somewhat surprised by the gesture.

"All the best," he replied, "I hope you find another job soon."

Ralph looked round for Peter. It was his turn for the noble gesture. He found him talking to Sam Clarke, the works shop steward.

"All the best Peter; Sam;" he said, shaking them both by the hand, "I hope you're not out of work too long."

"All the best Ralph," they replied in unison. Today everyone was in the same boat so old hatchets were buried.

Ralph disappeared into the street. He would have to reconcile his beliefs with reality.. Once the initial shock was over that would be done with consumate ease and faceless third parties, looking a bit like Peter and taking orders from Moscow, would be to blame.

Eventually the doors shut but the bar didn't. There wouldn't be many more good things for the gaffer to be on to.

Johnny looked about the bar. The dancing had stopped and a slow ballad crooned out of the juke box. He saw working people and shook his head in disbelief. He went over to Peter.

"Look here chap. We've just had a party. It ay anything to celebrate is it? All these folks just stuck on the scrap heap. Some of 'em will never work again. It's nothing to celebrate."

Peter looked his mate up and down before shaking his head ruefully. "Having a loff [laugh] at adversity has always been a working class trait. The posh folks day [didn't] create the Dunkirk Spirit even if it is them as is always bleating about it. That Dunkirk Spirit has always been there and that's what we've seen today."

Johnny reflected on Peter's words. 'The Dunkirk Spirit.' That's what it was, taking defeat and mocking it. Losing their livelihoods then having a party was mocking the defeat. It didn't matter, life could still be enjoyed.

It did matter though. When the shock was over and reality dawned on the hundreds of families affected by the closure of Newcombes it mattered; life was harder. Some found other jobs, the majority did.... eventually. Some asked the question; how could this be prevented from ever happening again.

THE BATS UNDER THE BELFRY

A bowl of Rice Krispies and tea from a mug devoid of a throstle and a hawthorn branch on the side - it was a few more years before my love affair with West Bromwich Albion manifested itself. Out into the grey Dudley morning and off to school. Kates Hill County Primary School, half-way up the hill. Cawney Bank looked down into the playground. The school looked down on the Woodlands old folks' home. Kates Hill was the universe then. Our fathers had been to all corners of the globe in World War Two but the world beyond Kates Hill was an unreal world, the grown-up's world, the world of television and the "flicks" and what did the grown-ups know about anything? They were worried about four "long-haired layabouts" called The Beatles and the increased difficulty they had caused in getting us to the barbers. Our microcosm was the real world and a relatively cosy world. Everest was the tallest mountain, the Empire State the tallest building, the Mississippi the longest river and Tarzan the strongest mon. (Or was it Samson that week?) Time was linear, not the getting-exponentially-shorter time of the adult.

Teachers were grown-ups and of that other world in which they talked of responsibilities. In our world too however there were those who had to shoulder responsibility. In the top class there were the prefects, so laden with responsibility that they were oft conceived as being on the other side. Then in each class was a milk monitor, a sports monitor and a librarian. Lapel badges in the school colours, bottle green and gold, were worn by the custodians of those proud offices. A simple M or S for the former two but the latter was written out in full as its possessor was supposed to have a more literary bent as he looked after the book cupboard which bore the grandiose title of the school library. The milk monitor carried the crate of third-pint milk bottles up to the classroom at morning playtime and he poked the holes in the top of each one with the special prodder someone's dad had made which even had a guard on it about an inch from the point. It was his responsibility also to return the empties. The sports monitor looked after the sports equipment and it was his job to get it ready for "games" when we would troop off down to Buffery Park. He also had to put it away tidily in its proper place when we trooped back. Its proper place was the little cubby hole situated below the bell tower. No one knew for sure whether it had ever housed a bell but the bell tower it was certainly was to us.

As we drifted back to school after dinner on that grey day, the sports monitor was the centre of attention. He'd been putting the equipment away as usual and the caretaker had gone up into the bell tower itself. What exactly happened couldn't be stated with any certainty, the story had gone through the school like wildfire. The caretaker had come down from the bell tower pretty sharpish and he'd "gone white with fright". Up in the darkness of the bell tower he'd seen a white hand. A grown-up had been frightened by a white hand in the bell tower!

In no time at all everyone knew this and the dominants worked on the possibilities and theories. Hands are connected to bodies so it was obvious that there was a body up there. That was the first conclusion. Then one of the more knowledgeable came out with, "If yoe stab yer 'ond, it guz white." The body in the bell tower had been stabbed and within minutes nearly two hundred kids were aware of the fact. The bloody hole right through the middle of the hand confirming the stab theory soon followed as did the hand trying to strangle the caretaker who, white faced and with hair standing on end, fled in terror. Had we known of the effects of adrenalin on the various sphincters at that stage, our descriptions of the poor chap would undoubtedly have stretched further.

The grown-up world was one of varying shades of grey. Two hundred adults might have had great difficulty in deciding what to do about a malevolent, stabbed, white hand lurking in the bell tower. Not so two hundred kids. Our world was still black and white - with the possible exception of Hercules cropping up from time to time to make the contest for the world's strongest mon a three 'oss race. It took no directive from up on high and no time at all for us to declare to a boy, "ah bay gooin up theer!" Simplicity itself. If the hand in the bell tower wanted revenge it wouldn't be collaring any of us. In those days the nagging thing about horror stories was the stupidity of the grown-up who would venture into a place infested with bogey men and the like. If the grown-up hadn't been stupid enough to enter the haunted house in the first place then no one would have ended up frightened. Only Doctor Who was allowed to do such things with impunity, he was after all a Time Lord and Daleks really weren't to be tolerated. They might come to Kates Hill!

The conclusion of dinner time was signalled by one of the teachers ringing a hand bell. We trooped off to our classrooms somewhat reluctantly. An atmosphere gripped the entire school, an atmosphere akin to that observed during thunderstorms. The atmosphere of collective fear when everything is conceived suddenly as being still, a time when we can taste each other's misgivings about the predicament. The clocks seem to tick louder and a dropping pin would clatter. Who could concentrate on classes in that situation. Things still had to be worked out. O.K. so none of us were venturing into the cubby hole let alone the bell tower but what if the body came down. If he's been murdered (sexists at the age of nine? The body was deemed male) then he won't rest until he has killed someone.

Those with classrooms upstairs gave the door to the cubby hole an accentuated wide berth. The unsuspecting were mercilessly sent careening towards the door by the bully element who were sworn at for their pains, fear having overridden fear. The apprehension was soon picked up by the teachers who wanted to know what on earth was the matter. Their glib dismissals of our theories as nonsense didn't carry any weight, we *knew* different. "Yoe ask the caretaker, he sid it." Talk of mass hysteria was still over a decade away but the teachers knew that here was something that had to be nipped in the bud. The much liked and respected teacher of the top class went up into the bell tower himself to disprove all the talk of bloody hands and bodies. We had no bookies' sons in our class but it was eleven to four the field that we'd never see him again. What a stout yeoman! "'E ay arf brave." Why couldn't the headmaster go up though. Two birds with one stone. We'd be rid of the headmaster and the body would have its revenge. The headmaster was obviously frightened, not up to the task. "'E ay brave, 'e con on'y stond up theer in the mornin' an' talk about it. Meks ya sick...."

The bookies mopped their brows in relief as the teacher from top class reappeared from the gloom of the bell tower. There was no body up there, no hand, no blood, nothing. It was all some flight of fancy, a story blown up out of all proportion. A theory that he had seen the body but was so brave that he hadn't let on was soon dismissed, not on the grounds that he wasn't that brave, but by virtue of the fact that "'E doe lie." After the news was broken the teachers allowed us a few minutes excited chatter before we simmered down. We all knew the score but couldn't discuss it until afternoon playtime.

Knowing full well the state of play, and it was obvious that the teachers didn't, we again gave the door to the cubby hole an accentuated wide berth on the way down to the playground. The fact of the matter was that the bell tower was haunted. The caretaker had seen no body for there was no body there. What he *had* seen was a ghost. The atmosphere dissipated somewhat and a malevolent hand was beginning to hold the credentials of an innocuous spectre. It was mooted that someone must have been murdered in the bell tower many years before, the school was after all built in 1874, and the victim's ghost had come back to haunt the place. So, ghosts were real after all. Ghosts didn't actually hurt anyone though, leastways not in our book. They simply haunted, walked abroad frightening people on purpose. That was a ghost's task in life, to frighten folks. That the caretaker had, a few hours before, escaped strangulation by a whisker was quickly forgotten. Fresh information had made that theory as dead as the dinosaurs. No one would get hurt now, only frightened. Despite this it was considered sound thinking to sleep with one's light on for that evening at any rate as a gloomy winter dusk descended on the Black Country......

"Greg! Greg! It's time to get up!"

It was indeed time to get up and it was Monday morning. A round of toast and tea from a mug adorned with a throstle and a hawthorn branch - my love affair with West Bromwich Albion was over a decade old. Life was no longer black and white. I had a job, exams to take for that job, taxes to pay, I loved a girl, did she love me? Politics to discuss, life to understand. Life was speeding up.

As I munched toast I asked my mother, "Do you remember the day we reckoned the bell tower up at Kates Hill was haunted?"

"No." she replied somewhat puzzled.

"I had a dream about it last night. I'd forgotten all about it."

The day after the bell tower scare it was as though nothing had happened. The incident had been forgotten as quickly as it had started. Completely forgotten.

I walked down to Fisher Street to catch the 87 into Birmingham. Seemingly I hadn't forgotten.

THE MINOR AND THE MINER'S SON

1) The Cup Run

The happy throngs milled around the "home of football". The London correspondents were wont to label Wembley Stadium thus since England's national side had won the World Cup there two years earlier. The blue and whites and the yellow and blues, an undulating sea of colour formed by hats, scarves, coats and banners. The air was one of expectancy for both sets of supporters. The game was still to be played, both teams were going to win the F.A. Cup Final, the carnival of the English sporting calendar. It was indeed a carnival atmosphere without the slightest hint of violence even from the very drunk.

There was a darker side. Touts sold tickets at vastly inflated prices and fanatical football fans were easy prey. Inside the stadium the spectacle would be witnessed by many people who wouldn't understand the rules of a game they had never seen live before. The clubs who had battled their way through the early rounds were given a meagre allocation of tickets all of which wouldn't necessarily reach the supporters. It was a prestige event with prestige people in attendance and much money to be made on the side. The supporters of Everton seemed more inclined to journey to London to pay a king's ransom to the touts in order to see the game but decked in the blue and white of West Bromwich Albion young Bobby Smith was a sad testimony to there being something wrong with the system.

It was getting late with the kick off barely thirty minutes away. Most people were inside the ground now but a few ran past him every now and again to get through the turnstiles in time. They were lucky, they had tickets. Poor Bobby wept unashamedly on the steps of Wembley for he would not get to see the game. He didn't even notice his father's consoling hand on his shoulder as he looked at his tiny watch, the face of which he'd scratched trying to emulate his hero Astle in the playground. The hard facts of the time and the crowd inside chanting "Astle is the king" made him cry all the more. Big hot tears ran down his freckled cheeks, it was a sad cruel world he thought as he scanned the north London skyline for some consolation but there could only be one consolation; a ticket to get inside. But F.A. Cup Final tickets didn't just materialise from the Wembley roof tops in the distance. He was the epitome of dejection. It was so grossly unfair. He'd seen all the other matches in the competition that far except the replay at Southampton which he couldn't possibly have gone to because of school. Oh yes and he'd missed the very first game in the third round at

Colchester but Albion had only been given a thousand tickets and nobody had had any inkling then of what was going to happen. The team had nearly come unstuck on that tiny ground but a last minute penalty gave them a replay in West Bromwich. Bobby's F.A. Cup started on that night when his heroes walked home easy winners. He'd seen the home tie with Southampton. There had been an element of luck on that occasion too but no one seemed overly perturbed by the thought of a replay and Bobby certainly wasn't perturbed at missing it, the idea hadn't jelled in anyone's mind yet, there still wasn't enough to go on.

The first flash across Bobby's mind that providence might have some bearing on things came with the announcement that the replay was to be televised. Confirmation of Divine intervention came with the result. Two goals to one behind with fifteen minutes to go and the goalkeeper off the park with concussion the Albion came back to win by three goals to two and the nation saw it. The murmurs of the latter day soothsayers gained much credence after that showing. All the ingredients were there, an element of luck to stay in the competition against inferior opposition, a fortuitous bounce of the ball to beat the goalkeeper in the next round. A side needed a bit of luck to win the F.A. Cup. A bit of luck and a lot of fight. The guts the whole side had shown at Southampton had proved that the team had the necessary fight in them. There could be no doubt about it, the F.A. Cup would be coming to West Bromwich that year. Bobby lapped up the whispered mystical chatter in the crowd in the following league match. Everybody seemed to realise, there were many confident nods of knowing heads.

Robert Smith senior wasn't in the least bit interested in football. He never had been and he never would be but he took his son Bobby to all the games at the Hawthorns and to the more important away fixtures. Bobby had been indifferent to football until the World Cup competition of 1966. After that he, like many other boys who hadn't previously bothered, became actively interested. Living in the businessman's belt of Sutton Coldfield he had three choices as to which team to follow; Birmingham City, Aston Villa and West Bromwich Albion. Birmingham City were in the second division at that stage and Aston Villa were floundering in the first. West Bromwich had, he learnt, won the League Cup the previous season and his grandfather had supported them since the previous century so the choice had not been completely arbitrary. From the day he made his choice Bobby came to love his team to such an extent that his moods mirrored the fortunes of the side. Robert senior quite enjoyed the weekend diversion, it took his mind off the troubles of his business week, but he didn't pretend to know the rules or who played in the teams. He learnt enough however to drop the odd name to business colleagues who did take an interest and many did because football was a boom industry. England was relatively prosperous, the world cup generated and regenerated interest in the game and crowds again flocked to the grounds as they had done just after the war. Above all the grounds were relatively safe, more and more women were attending and the occasional battles between rival "kop choirs" smacked of rivalry rather than viciousness. Grounds were open, in some the fans could pay at one end and walk round to the other unchallenged. There were no fences around the track so that hundreds of young boys ran on to the pitch at the end of a game eager to just touch one of their heroes. It seemed quite healthy. Fathers would take their sons to stand where they had stood, it was the national game and one to be proud of.

Robert Smith senior took his son in the main stand. They didn't have season tickets because going to football matches was still only experimental in his eyes. They did however manage to get in more or less the same spot for every game as Robert got his tickets from business associates. With the away games he was generally able to procure good seats through contacts in various parts of the country. Very few games had been all ticket however so his contacts both home and away had yet to be tested. The fifth round brought a tie on the south coast against the once great team of Portsmouth who were then in the second division. This was the first all ticket affair and had proved no problem. Bobby was quite worried when they hadn't any tickets with just a few days to go before the tie, they hadn't a season ticket and his father refused point blank to queue up outside the ground as the majority had to. He came up trumps however with seats in the centre stand. He could, he told his son, have got any old ticket any old time he wished but he wanted the best seats and got them. Bobby had to admit to doubting his father's ability when time was running out but his procuring of two quality seats gave him a blind mystical faith that his dad could do anything.

The victory at Pompey by two goals to one earned the team a home draw in the sixth round against mighty Liverpool. Again it was all ticket and again Robert Smith came up with the tickets for the goalless draw, which meant yet another all ticket game, the replay at Anfield. No one went to Anfield to do anything further than participate. To the rest of the country Albion's cup run was at an end. No one who had anything to do with West Bromwich Albion in any capacity was in the least bit perturbed at the prospect, it all seemed preordained, it added a touch of drama to the plot. Bobby was on his Easter holidays from school and so was able to attend the game. Robert hadn't been able to obtain centre stand tickets this time but he came up with some seats in amongst a ruck of West Bromwich supporters in the wing of the stand which overlapped the Kop. They were isolated and surrounded by hostility as the bulk of the travelling fans were at the other end of the ground. Throughout the game that tiny band were pelted with a range of missiles including bottles and paper cups into which the Scousers had urinated. Liverpool took the lead and the Fleet Street hacks composed I told you so reports on the game for their respective journals. The noise that the small band made got to the reportedly good natured Kop more so than the thousands at the other end of the field, they didn't believe that all was lost and they wouldn't shut up. Midway through the second half Astle rose to a cross from the right wing and headed the equaliser at the Kop end. He ran to the corner of the ground to salute that small group of Albion fans. To Bobby it was the equivalent of receiving a telegram from the Queen. By the end of extra time the name of Albion was to emblazon the morning copy. Even Robert had been sufficiently moved by the event to shout at the top of his voice, albeit a threat of violence, to the Scouse urchins who persisted in throwing missiles. Bobby noted his fathers open expression of emotion with a tinge of pride, he was after all a dad to be proud of.

Robert saw to the tickets for the second replay the following day. He wanted to witness the exit of the northern animals, which was his new view of Liverpool, from the F.A. Cup. He took his son to that match and they both enjoyed the 2 - 1 victory which ensured an all Midlands semi-final against Birmingham City at Villa Park. That second replay at Maine Road in Manchester had been a classic cup battle with Albion's left half, John Kaye, playing most of the match with his head bandaged like an Apache. Again it seemed scripted with the local derby resulting from all the excitement.

With the semi-final in town Robert could have earned a comfortable living as a tout from all the tickets that were put his way. He took only the two he needed. Albion this time were expected to win and they did so in a low key affair. Things had gone according to script however, West Bromwich Albion were on their way to Wembley.

Robert's business was picking up too. A big deal was in the offing with a major French company. He was starting to put feelers out for tickets to the great occasion. He hadn't got any concrete offers but was quietly confident that the goods would come from somewhere when a hiccup in negotiations with the French meant that he had to go to Paris in person to iron things out.

The final was fast approaching and the negotiations dragged on and on. Bobby retained faith in his father's ability to obtain tickets right up until the final week when there was still no sign of his return from Paris. With an air of confidence he told his friends at school that he would be there for the culmination of four month's drama. Even on the day before the big game the thought that he wouldn't witness the spectacle in person was so unreal that he couldn't entertain it. His father returned from Paris late on the Friday afternoon and immediately phoned the man who had supplied his tickets throughout the season. The look on his face as he put down the receiver conveyed the message to Bobby. No Cup Final after all he'd seen! At once his young life seemed to be without meaning.

Robert realised what it meant to his son. He made quick calculations. He was low on cash and had missed the banks but he could take Bobby down to Wembley and, if he found a generous tout, he would be able to buy him a ticket. It meant that Bobby would have to go into the ground on his own, an idea which didn't appeal to him greatly but getting that far was highly improbable as the notion of a generous tout was in his view ridiculous. That people who profited from other people's love would fall for a sob story stood no reason. He told Bobby his plan however and it must have sounded convincing because he went to bed quietly confident that he would see his team at Wembley on the morrow.

They went to London early the following day and Robert soon came to realise that his finances didn't stretch to the asking price of even a terrace ticket. There were plenty of Merseysiders around who were "soccer mad" enough to keep the market buoyant. He couldn't stop trying however and must have walked around the stadium four times. Robert felt that he had asked every tout in London but there were no cut-price tickets and the minutes ticked by. Robert and Bobby stood on the steps, further walking and asking seemed futile. Robert promised Bobby that they would have season tickets the following year and that he would take him to all the away games. He would see to it that he met all the players. Why, he'd be an intimate of Astle himself before very long. Robert felt much of the despair of his son as he reeled out his promises. He felt angry that he had let such a situation develop. He also felt a sense of impotence as he was, for once, powerless to do anything about it. Bobby wasn't listening. He thought of all the previous rounds and how meaningless his future life would be because he had missed what it had all been for; the F.A. Cup Final at Wembley. He was completely within himself, the epitome of utter wretchedness. People running by with tickets cast sympathetic glances towards him. Some smiled reassuringly but they too were powerless to alter his plight. Bobby payed them no mind. The only truth was the depth of his despair.

2) The Saint On The Steps

It was a carnival to be sure but Ron Westwood wasn't altogether convinced that he should be attendant at such an event. It was too soon. His father had been a miner and he was a miner's son. Ron was a miner too but even if he had been a London based writer he would still have been a miner's son, the connection with the pit community was irrevocable. The male line of the family had been face cutters in the south Staffordshire coalfields as far back as was traceable. The men had followed the fortunes of West Bromwich Albion since before anyone cared to remember.

Ron would miss his father. He had been a good man, well respected in the community; the union, the club, the neighbourhood. They had been through a lot together, at work and at play, not least of which was going to the Hawthorns. He had been a good story teller, a natural raconteur with a ready wit which he frequently peppered with grass roots political philosophy. He used to tell how early on in his working life he had faced the troops sent by Churchill to Cannock Chase in the General Strike. The one rancorous cross he bore throughout his life had been his hatred of the Nottinghamshire miners for the part they played in undermining that conflict with their formation of the Spencer Union. To him it was unforgivable blindness on their part to tow the Tory line against their comrades in the mining industry in particular and the whole of the working class in general. He never visited that county as a result and on one occasion took a hundred mile detour so as not to cross the border. Ron always looked on this quirk of his fathers as a touch of eccentricity. The rest of his political thinking he deemed as being most sound, but Ron hadn't lived through the schismatic times of the General Strike. He had been born just before the war and his earliest memories were of the blackout. His formative years were spent in the company of socialists who were committed to carving out the New Jerusalem from the ashes of a world war. The impetus was lost somewhere along the way and he became a man in the consumer boom of the 1950s. The working class seemed to have developed a soft underbelly as it wallowed on the soft mattress of materialism. Despite the ups and downs inherent in the capitalist system, the age of consumerism continued on into the 1960s. There was a lot of work around and people had money in their pockets. They were indeed exciting as well as prosperous times in which to live. The young generation's explosive creativity was questioning the establishment in new ways. Of the world's capital cities, London was the place to be in the 'sixties. Ron knew no other England, the England of his father's recollections seemed unimaginable to him.

His father's tales had more than a hint of parable about them. Many of his generation talked of the harsh times of the past as though there was something glorious about them and the people who survived them. It was the stock method of proving the worthlessness of modern youth who lacked discipline and had it so easy. Ron's father's recollections always seemed to carry a message far deeper than the glib denigration of of the young generation. Everything he said came across as though each sentence had been carefully considered. Ron would recollect his father with pride though he knew he would never be able to emulate his word power or delivery.

Walking along Wembley Way Ron recalled one of his father's last pieces of mysterious wisdom. Coming off the shift that afternoon he had casually dropped it out.

"Coming up the Albion tonight son?"

Ron was bemused at first, then alarmed. If his father mentioned a game then there was sure to be one on but he was certainly unaware of it. He was soon enlightened.

"The reserves have got a game on. Stafford Rangers in the Staffordshire Senior Cup."

There seemed to be an urgency in his delivery implying that they were going whatever Ron might have to say on the matter.

"I'd like to bet they'll be issuing vouchers for cup tickets tonight." He added mysteriously. In Ron's mind there was no bet about it and yes they were going to the Albion.

Sure enough they were issued with a green voucher when they passed through the turnstiles and this ensured them tickets for the three games against Liverpool, the semi-final against Birmingham City and, far more important than could be imagined, the final tie against Everton. In retrospect, equating the attendance at a reserve game in a minor competition with certain qualification for a Cup Final ticket seemed totally absurd but Ron's father had seen the equation long before it had any meaning.

He only had two years to go until his retirement and was as active physically as he was mentally. His death had come as a complete shock to everyone even though premature departures from the earthly sojourn were not uncommon in mining communities. Pneumosilicosis wasn't the registered cause of death but it was a lung related problem which brought it about. He died within a week of the onset of the illness and didn't suffer unduly. Ron was thankful of that and remembered the last time he saw him alive. He had asked Ron to pass him his wallet from his bedside locker. He seemed to fumble as his movements were very jerky but he eventually managed to pull out the treasured Final ticket. He handed it to Ron and told him, "Give it to someone as deserves." It was almost the last thing he said to his son.

The funeral had been on the Thursday, two days before the Final. They should have been going to Wembley together, his foresight had put the tickets in their pockets. Even he had no way of foreseeing that it wasn't to be. Ron was in a state of shock and really in two minds about going but come the morning of the match some of his mates from the colliery prised him out of the house and on to the coach to Wembley. A few beers on the way down helped to displace the sick empty feeling he held within but it would never go away completely. They were nearing the gate and Ron had completely forgotten about he spare ticket in his wallet. The sight of Bobby moved Ron; life went on, people still had strong emotions. Here was this kid, outside of his family his football team was probably the only thing he ever cared about in his life, the first thing he'd probably ever loved, and in his all-consuming love he'd reckon that he'd let his team down by not being able to get inside the ground to spur them on. Love is blind, thought Ron; the club had let the boy down, just because he hadn't been to an obscure reserve game or didn't possess a season ticket...... He remembered that extra ticket.

Robert Smith detected the subtle change of course that brought Ron towards them. Robert's face was expressionless, he didn't dare so much as hope, Bobby had been hurt enough as it was. Bobby himself had ceased to notice anything.

It all happened so quickly. Ron pulled the ticket from his wallet and Robert pulled out his wallet too. He was incredulous when the money he offered was waved away. Ron ruffled Bobby's hair which broke his trance. He looked up to see a hand holding a ticket out to him. It couldn't be true, it had to be a dream. Or were prayers really answered? The face at the end of the arm was simple, it held a sadness, but it conveyed an understanding. Bobby knew that its owner was on his side.

"Here son, the Baggies are going to bring that silver pot back," Ron said. He shook the ticket as he knew that Bobby was unsure what was going on. When the full impact of the gesture dawned on him his face lit up. He would never forget the face at the end of the arm, it was the face of a saint. He humbly took the ticket as though it was from a saint. His hand was shaking violently, he didn't want the precious item to disappear. He couldn't say any words of thanks, he had lost his power of speech. Ron turned and hurried to catch his friends. Robert Smith was thanking him heartily as he went.

With the instructions where to meet after the game firmly implanted father and son parted. Bobby sprinted to the turnstiles. He saw the great spectacle. He saw Astle find the net early on in the first period of extra time to ensure the cup was taken back to West Bromwich. He saw the team parade the cup through West Bromwich High Street from an open top bus. There was no way that he would ever forget the face that had made that possible. There was no way that he could ever thank its bearer enough, or indeed ever repay him.

3) 1984 - West Bromwich

Much ado had been made at the start of the year about George Orwell's last novel. How well would the real year compare with the author's fictional 1984? Throughout the year, newspaper editorials constantly referred to the work though the initial popular interest soon petered out. The inclusions more often than not had something to do with the miner's strike which began early in the year.

Ron Westwood was thinking.

The England of 1984 was certainly different to that of 1948 when the novel was written. The West Bromwich of 1984 probably had more in common with the town of 1948 than with the town of 1968 which welcomed back the cup heroes. In 1968 there had been hope in that town as there had been across the nation; school leavers could expect to find employment which would give them a secure financial base, the town didn't have the spectre of mass unemployment over it. Similarly the town of 1948 had the hope of a rosy future, the war was over and Europe lived in peace. The gradual recovery from the war years however meant that the times of 1948 were austere; but at least there was the hope of better things to come. The town of 1984 again had the bleakness of austerity about it. The colourful neo-Victorian-cum-Fanny-by-a-gaslight facades of shops that were the contemporary vogue couldn't hide the fact, they could indeed have been the product of the austerity that went hand in glove with a life without hope. Splashes of paint were the only thing to brighten a sad existence in all the towns which had a high percentage of unemployment and great uncertainty about the jobs that were. The land of hope and glory was a nation divided, it was becoming mother of only those free enough to pay for it. Never had the right been so ruthless and uncaring, never had the left been seemingly so impotent. The right had all the tools at its disposal, national dailies could lie with impunity. The tool of the left, the working class itself, had gone soft through years of apparent prosperity without any real shift in the balance of power. Brains had been adled into a blinkered view of things and unions became near-as-damn-it Tories in only seeking short term financial gains for their members. The electorate voted in 1983 for more from the gospel of the self which meant that the wings of the trade union movement were about to be clipped. Large sections of the working class were suffering but there was no fight back, they had lost their teeth from too much sugar and the subtle propaganda of the establishment.

The miners had always been regarded as the vanguard of the proletariat by the extreme left and were feared by the right because Conservative governments had been brought down in their wake. The pre-Falklands Thatcher, figure of great unpopularity, had refused to take them on over the question of pit closures. The post-Falklands, post-election Thatcher, figure of great esteem, decided that the time in early 1984, was right. The strike became the most divisive in British industrial history. It was called by the national executive of the N.U.M., there had been no ballot. Under the rules of the union, the democratically elected executive were empowered to do that. The media cried wolf, the N.U.M. were throwing the country into a turmoil and they were doing it undemocratically. The nation was up in arms. The lack of a ballot became the centre of attention rather than the Coal Boards hit list of pits. The N.U.M. conference came and went and the section in the rule book that empowered the executive to call a strike without a ballot stood unchallenged by the democratic process of that union. Still the strike was dubbed undemocratic by and the leadership vilified. An Act of Parliament curbing trade union "power" enabled a High Court injunction to be served on the strikers by a group of working miners. There were working miners, a fair number of them. In Nottinghamshire the strike was only token, there were no Nottinghamshire pits earmarked for closure. The politics of he self had corrupted the vanguard itself. There had been violent clashes on the picket lines, arson, and even death as the strike edged towards Christmas. The gradual drift back to work in the solid areas brought about by attrition was increased by nothing short of an out and out bribe by the bosses.

Ron's thoughts depressed him. He stood with two colleagues, a brazier, some placards and a collection bucket in West Bromwich High Street. No cars passed through that section now, an inner ring road surrounded the town centre. Even the name of the town had changed, it was now officially called Sandwell. Ron mused over the changes there had been and the present situation regarding the strike. Had his father been right about Nottinghamshire? They were collecting precious little other than abuse. Television pictures were shown in which hoardes of policemen in riot gear with truncheons drawn charged up streets. Exactly what they were running at was never clearly shown. Policemen carrying crates of milk bottles filled with clear liquid were reported as having confiscated petrol bombs. From whom or whence was only intimated. There was no film of one being thrown. By and large, the suggestions made were believed and the strikers were held to be an unruly mob. The undoubted acts of violence perpetrated by a tiny minority which did occur were blown up out of all proportion. The ethics of the union leadership and Labour politicians were called into question. The miners had neither the support of the middle class nor the majority of the working class.

The way the strike was reported on the continent was somewhat different. The pre-condition of a violent conflict that there are two opposing factions was displayed. European newsreels showed the other side of the coin.

4) 1984 - Athens

Bobby Smith was now virtually in control of the business of which his father had been a director in the 'sixties. His father had retired a few years earlier through ill health, leaving Bobby to the rigours of running a business, rigours that weren't without compensation. Bobby went on many business trips abroad, trips laced with pleasure. He believed he was entitled to his pleasure as he believed he was one of the elite. He assumed superiority over those of his countrymen who were neither businessmen nor of a "respectable" standing in the community. He assumed a superiority over all foreigners. He derided the working class for their stupidity, superstition and greed while adhering to the mythology of his own kind, the introspection and the greed. He questioned nothing.

Bobby had just completed a transaction in Athens and had decided on a few days rest to take in the sights. He was roaming Omonia Square in the early evening, pondering what to do next. The smell of food and a gnawing hunger led him into a bar. It was a small back street establishment which catered mainly for workers. The display counter was at the far end of the room. Bobby scanned the array of sausages, cheeses, and what looked to him like hot-pots. He made his order. He understood no Greek but the proprietor spoke a reasonable, if heavily accentuated, English. He sat at a vacant table and looked around. There were half a dozen tables in all and most of them were surrounded by men wearing overalls who were drinking beer. Their chatter was hearty and noisey and it obscured the drone from the television set behind the counter which no one seemed to be watching. The place was clean but dingy in appearance and spartan in decor. The proprietor, a rotund and apparently jovial character, served Bobby his food and beer at a time when he was starting to feel distinctly ill at ease. The smell of food and his rumbling stomach had attracted him there. The all too proletarian nature of the establishment and his natural sensibilities were starting to repel him. He felt that he stuck out like a sore thumb. But, the meal was now in front of him. It would soon be eaten and he could then ensconce himself somewhere more to his taste.

Contrary to his paranoia, the men at the other tables didn't pay him any mind. The television news began. The owner had tried to engage Bobby in conversation but had been treated with indifference. Bobby was relieved when he returned behind the counter. He watched the news as he ate, not understanding a word of it. Suddenly the landscape became familiar. A group of British policemen with truncheons drawn were chasing a solitary man. He was losing ground. On being caught he was dragged to the ground forcibly and continuously kicked, punched and beaten with truncheons. The proprietor no longer seemed jovial. He pointed to the screen and shouted over to one of the groups of men. He was gesticulating violently. The group became animated and grunted what Bobby took to be abuse at the screen. Bobby wasn't quite sure what the report was about, nor was he particularly bothered about its content, but the fact that the Greeks were becoming so animated about an item of news pertaining to Britain annoyed him considerably. If it was taking place in Britain then it was none of their business. The proprietor again tried to engage Bobby in conversation, though this time it came over as a lecture.

"They are trying to break your miners' union. Your police, very bad. Margaret Thatcher is crazy," he spat.

Bobby realised then that the report was about the miners strike. He was incensed, the Greek television was trying to portray the British police as being brutal. This just wasn't true! It wasn't on British television or in the papers. The police were just doing their job and yet the miners were perpetrating all kinds of acts against them. Bobby jumped to his feet. His complexion was crimson, he was absolutely livid.

"Now you look here!" he bawled at the owner who was immediately towering above him. "You can't just lie like that!"

The owner seemed to become calm when he simply grinned and said "Can't break unions, this Thatcher is crazy. You vote for her? Why people vote for her? She just crazy."

As though colonialism were innate, this was more than Bobby could stomach. He was having no foreigners telling him how to vote. Who did they think they were? His rapidly disappearing decorum finally snapped. He pushed the owner away forcibly, bawling obscenities centring around the fact that he was Greek and that his cuisine was different than was found in England. Bobby was beside himself with rage and didn't really know what he was doing physically, but the insults seemed to flow out as though they were often used, or often thought.

The owner was in no physical danger but the men rushed from the table to his assistance. They grabbed Bobby from behind and hurled him to the floor raining punches and kicks into him. The owner picked him out from the melee and dragged him onto the pavement outside, making sure his head hit the door on the way through. Bobby was flat on his back in the gutter peering up at the Athenian evening sky. In the doorway the mob stood for a few seconds to mouth Greek obscenities before returning to consume their beers passively as though nothing had happened.

After a few minutes a solitary man at one of the tables paid his bill and left. Bobby was still dazed in the gutter, though by now he was sitting up surveying the damage - to property moreso than person. He was wondering what had hit him and silently cursing the foreigners for attacking him from behind. The man leaving the café went straight over to help him up. He held Bobby steady as he dusted himself off. He started muttering about the hole in his brand new pair of trousers. Bobby was being told that he should be more concerned about the hole in his head that had been brought about by his collision with theedge of the door when he realised that the man who had come to his aid was English. He was at once exasperated.

"You.....you should have helped me in there," he blustered.

The frank reply he got disquieted him.

"I happen to agree with them, we're being shovelled a load of crap in England," he said sternly before adding, with more than a hint of accusation, "And people like you believe every word of it."

Bobby instinctively wanted to argue but felt that he couldn't do so rationally at that point. He still felt a little betrayed by the lack of patriotic loyalty the gentleman had displayed whatever his politics might be. The question "Would you have helped a striking miner in a similar situation?" put a stop to Bobby even contemplating taking the matter any further.

He was helped back to his hotel where he cleaned himself up. After a medical examination and X-rays to prove that no bones were broken he caught the first available flight to England.

He recounted the tale over a business lunch in a restaurant in an indoor shopping complex just off West Bromwich High Street. His face was no longer swollen but it carried a bruise, and his ribs were still sore. He took his client on from the restaurant to a wine bar where they drank enough to be in keeping with the spirit of Christmas which was barely a week away. As alcohol levels increased Bobby became increasingly animated on the subject of the miners strike. He now felt very much a part of the battle himself rather than a mere onlooker as he had the scars to prove it. They ordered a further bottle, the statutary one for the road. Bobby continued his invective right up until the time they left.

5) The Minor And The Miner's Son

Ron Westwood and his two colleagues continued their lonely picket in the pedestrian zone. The death of a taxi driver in South Wales had damaged the miners' cause considerably, bringing open hostility to the strikers. Most people walked past them as though they didn't exist. Some glared hostility for a while before going about their business. A few were openly abusive and even fewer were throwing money into the bucket. In the light of what had happened, those who were sympathetic didn't want to be seen to be so. The three were stamping their feet and blowing into cupped hands to keep out the chill. An old man wearing a grey mackintosh with a poppy still in the lapel broke away from his two cronies. He went up to Ron and started to bawl abuse.

"You lot are a bloody disgrace!" he shouted, angry at the violence and now death that surrounded the strike.

Ron too was very angry, angry and sad. He was sad that someone had been killed and angry because it gave fuel to the arguments that the propaganda machine had been putting all along. It made their position almost indefensible against an already hostile people. The old man ranted on and on, louder and louder.

The previous day Ron had returned to Cannock from the picket to find that the house in which toys that had been collected for the children of striking miners were stored had been broken into. The toys all donated by well-wishers, had been systematically destroyed. There had been money in the house too, but that had been left alone. It was an act of premeditated violence, an attempt to break the spirit of the striking miners through their children. The story made the local media but received no noticeable coverage nationally. This angered Ron as there was ready talk of intimidation of working miners in areas where the strike was solid, but in the south Staffordshire field the majority of men were in work and the converse happened. He, and strikers in other working areas, knew only too well that this went on but the rest of the population didn't know, or were kept from knowing.

Ron's temper got the better of him and he told the old man to shut his mouth because he was ignorant and he didn't know half of what was going on. He managed to physically control himself however as two policemen were in constant surveillance of the picket. They began walking over as the old man started flailing out at Ron. Ron was able to evade the onslaught quite easily and restrained his instinct to retaliate. He urged his two colleagues not to so much as move, arrests would be made in one quarter only. The old man's two friends pulled him away and tried to quieten him down. The two policemen were moving briskly towards the incident.

Bobby and his client witnessed the whole scene from a distance of some twenty five yards. They were both merry but their vision was far from hazy. It seemed that the three miners were to be arrested.

"That'll put a smile on your face," the client said to Bobby, but he wasn't listening.

It was him, there could be no mistaking that face. Obviously he was older and his face more lived-in, but, strangely, it seemed less sad than it was on that day outside Wembley all those years ago. He seemed to look resigned, as though years of experience had taught him something. At one point he smiled and laughed with the policeman. All this puzzled Bobby who eventually reasoned that as he knew nothing of the man he couldn't possibly explain anything about him or the expressions he exuded. It was ironic; the one person in the world whom he had never been able to repay in some way for a service rendered was part of a group that he loathed to the extent of stripping from them their human identity. The group were to be hated, the individuals who made the group were quite unimaginable as such. For the first time Bobby saw a member of that group as an individual, a human being with a past, a present and a future. And it was the individual to whom he would be forever indebted, the saint who had appeared out of the blue to get him into Wembley.

Bobby felt strange but had decided on what to do. He marched resolutely towards the miners. The client tried to stop him as he thought that Bobby was about to do something stupid. But Bobby was not to be stopped. The policemen weren't going to make any arrests and they had moved away as Bobby reached Ron. He threw a fifty pound note into the bucket much to the surprise of all three. He then shook Ron's hand and said simply,

"Thankyou, that's for you and your family this Christmas."

In Ron's palm had been placed a further fifty pounds. He was taken aback by what was clearly a very personal exchange. The "thankyou" left him puzzled. Before he had time to collect his wits and express his gratitude Bobby had disappeared round the corner with his client. The other two miners were highly delighted at the fifty pounds in the bucket and wanted to know who the benefactor was. Ron looked at the fifty in his hand and let that drop into the bucket as he muttered something about a friend from way back. He couldn't quite place it but he had a queer vision of a boy crying on some steps. It was all very hazy but he felt sure it had something to do with his father.

Bobby continued to berate the strikers in the company of his associates. Once a week he sent a substantial cheque to the strike fund. Ron continued to berate the Nottinghamshire miners in public. Some said he was getting to be like his old man on that subject. In moments of private reflection Ron would think how the world had changed since his father had died. He'd think how the Albion were in decline, how they could do with another Astle to reverse the tide. Then he'd remind himself that Astle had been plucked from a Nottinghamshire colliery to play football. Astle was the king. It wouldn't matter where the new one came from; even a Nottinghamshire colliery.

ON LEAVE

The white clock face shone frailly in the hoary January night. The heavy black hands pointed to barely discernible Roman numerals indicating a time which bore no relationship to the hour of the day. A black cat moving silently, sleekly, came to a halt. She looked up at the spire as though seeking inspiration then stared sullenly across the graveyard.

The moon was hidden but a few stars maintained their aloof sparkle. An occasional gust of wind blew to disturb the bare shrubs and the grass between the headstones of the strangely paradoxical plot of land caught behind sad iron railings, the guardians of a gothic facade. The scene was both tranquil and disturbing, neat yet unkempt, the stalks of last summer's remembrance rattling in stone chalices above the tombs, and the stark branches waving anarchicly at the ordered rows of distant death. The moon cast a beam momentarily through the clouds which glinted in the eyes of the prowler who stalked, once more, stealthily from tomb to tomb.

Behind me a few motor cars passed by wending their anonymous ways home. A bolt shut sharply, almost belligerently, declaring that the public house was now dead too until a new morning breathed fresh life through its doors. I could hear a faint crackle followed by even fainter electronic voices. A policeman was communicating with someone somewhere. The cat had come to rest near the railings through which I peered on a tomb which was more of a statement. It was a square stone slab with a simple stone cross some two feet in height. The cat stared at me as though he was anxious for my attention. When positive of its possession he blinked down at the inscription. I read without excitement as a feeling that any capacity for emotion had been taken from me grew within. The concepts of time and space seemed to have flown as I picked my way from word to word. They were twins. To be born on the same day was a prerequisite of the condition, to die on the same day hinted at something tragic, perhaps even sinister. I felt no sense of that tragedy nor even remotely inquisitive. the twins had died on the same night, I had taken it as read, strangely read, as I gave them an identity and assumed that they had died in the cold of the night.

Something deep inside told me that it had gone oddly cold, or maybe I had gone cold. With no points of reference it was difficult to tell which was true. The unobtrusive shuffling of gravel beneath leather and the wierd sense of a presence a few yards away.... an old man had come to look into the past. I knew he was old but I didn't turn round to confirm this, it simply was.

In resumed preoccupation I stared through the railings which seemed suddenly heavier yet more ornate. Snow covered the ground, and with a host of people milling around the scene was reminiscent in some respects of Bruegel's "Hunters in the Snow", though the immediate townscape had a definite Lowrian aspect. Sharp featured people in well worn clothes trudged up a hill, their backs bent over as though the very act of walking was symbolic of the drudgery of their lives. There was a bridge across a deep cutting in which there was a railway station. From the crevice exuded a cacophony of chatter, both human and mechanical, billows of grey smoke, and the coal-stained smell of the steam engine. There was a hissing, a whistle, a clattering of wheels; the trail of smoke was broken as the engine passed beneath the bridge bound for Birmingham or Worcester. A little way up the hill crowds gathered outside the music hall. I could sense poverty in the way they dressed but there was laughter and a certain stoic dignity about them which suggested a genuine sense of humour rather than the forced gaiety of a brave face. The doors opened and they filed in.

Horses snorted hot breath which condensed in the chill pulled carts. Other steeds rested with nosebags hung about their snouts, chewing contentedly, warily watching the world go by. Trams rattled by filled with people, acetylene lamps flickered and wisps of smoke wafted from a brazier in the corner. A small boy in clothes too thin for the inclemency of the winter night shouted shrill, incomprehensible headlines into the wind. The child had rickets and would never know of war. A motor car drew to a halt, its coachwork gleamed and the ornate silver radiator cast distorted reflections of the scene into dulled faces. A well-groomed young man alighted and bought a paper from the lad who doffed his cap like an automaton. It didn't seem in the least bit odd that I recognised the young man. He looked in my direction before returning to the car. I knew he hadn't seen me, it was as though I wasn't there at all. The car pulled away. They were going to a village called Gornal, that much I knew.

I surveyed again the Lowrian townscape; the factories and chimneys, the rows of houses caked in grime, the gas lamps glowing, casting light on the darkness and invoking a feeling of warmth and unity. At the top of the hill a Norman keep overshadowed all in the vicinity to give the whole an element of fantasy.

The castle receded into the background looking a ridiculous incongruity. It had no business in the picture as I focused on the man selling potatoes and chestnuts from the brazier. He was watching me closely and I felt uneasy. I felt; that in itself seemed strange. His heavy overcoat kept out the chill where there were no holes. He wore a felt cap beneath which an aquiline nose and a ruddied complexion compounded a gaunt but timeless expression. He alone would survive the sombre figures trudging onwards all around him, he alone would march forward into the painting or the prose, he was a poet who knew no verse, nor cared. We spoke endlessly without exchanging any words as the night drifted on.

Across the road was a pond which had frozen over. The children who had been playing on the ice all evening were drifting home, the ragged urchins who were busy learning, learning how to laugh despite it all. They had no skates nor had they needed any. Two boys remained. They had skates, they were better clothed and looked better fed. Both were handsome in features and appeared jolly though this could have been less than genuine. They were twins and knew only each other. Camaraderie went without skates.

The streets filled up again as the music hall had finished and the public houses were turning out. The last train pulled into the station and its passengers joined the confusion of the crowd. A sailor coming home on leave was carrying his bag over his shoulder. His greatcoat alone seemed adequate for the weather. Hardened by North Sea gales he alone seemed unperturbed, he alone stood tall, walked tall, he alone had a visible burden. People were milling, moving quickly, moving slowly, huddling in tight knots gossiping, the show, the job, the neighbours, a confusing mass of humanity. There was a scream followed by a general commotion, people were running, seemingly everywhere, but only in one direction.

The ice in the middle of the pond had cracked and given way under the weight of one of the twins. His brother skated towards the circle of black water into which he had disappeared. The whole surface of the pond was beginning to fracture into a flotilla of ice boats. The body came to the surface. He had died instantly as the insidious shock of the gelid, dark mere struck him. His brother stood and gazed fixedly at the corpse bobbing in the water. A number of people were watching in silence by now as the section on which he was standing broke away and tilted cruelly. He lost his balance and slid to his inevitable doom, slowly but surely, as onlookers screamed at the horror and their own helplessness.

Everyone was now running towards the scene of the tragedy, or away from it to tell of it. The man at the brazier stood his ground and viewed the tapestry with an air of detachment. Over the centuries he had seen the like on many occasions. I found myself running with the crowd. The man at the brazier watched me, he was shaking his head. I stopped exactly where I was, he was quite right.

The boy was floundering in the ice-cold water near the still figure of his dead twin. He was screaming. He could see his short life sinking out of his grasp. He stretched his arms towards the crowd on the bank and, seeking salvation, looked imploringly at the faces. The faces in turn hoped that he would escape his panic and make the bank safely. Everyone was thinking how unsure they were in the water themselves, and it was ice-cold too..... but maybe someone in the crowd could..... They all remained silent however, mesmerised by their collective impotence. No one had come to effect a rescue, no one had come to play the hero's lead, no one had set out that night to watch a small boy die a hopeless, helpless death. There were people all around the edge of the pool now and they would remain until the show was over, until the child sank for the last time. Someone held out a stick but it was far too short and the gesture was derided for its inevitable failure rather than applauded for its naked sublimity. All seemed lost, a priest in the crowd prayed for the deliverance of the boys' souls, the crowd prayed for a reprieve as the truth began to dawn.

There was a stir of activity on the far side of the pond. The erect man of the sea had cast his kitbag and greatcoat to the ground. Excited murmurs rang round the circle as he dived into the black abyss, there was hope after all. The priest thanked The Lord while the crowd cheered the sailors every stroke. He was a strong swimmer and soon reached the boy who was no longer aware of anything. There was a loud hurrah as he held the boy in his arms and started for the bank. The cheer turned to a gasp of incredulity. Pain was written clearly across the sailor's face as cramp froze his limbs. It was all over in a moment. The seaman sank to a sailor's death though he was far from any ocean. The twins shared death as they had shared birth. The crowd looked on in disbelief, some joined priest in prayer.

The police arrived to disperse the crowd and the fire brigade to retrieve the bodies. The bodies of the boys were in the morgue before the last knots of people broke up to go home. The body of the sailor was never found. Only the man at the brazier had viewed the proceedings with the necessary detachment to tell the young men in the motor car on their return from Gornal exactly what the all too apparent commotion was about. His version became the lore. Only the sailor had the wherewithal to play the heroic lead, or a kharma preventing him playing any other role. He became part of the lore.

The young man I knew bought a bag of chestnuts. He was looking in my direction and again he hadn't seen me. The man at the brazier smiled reassuringly. he seemed to be saying that it was time for me to go home, as though I knew where home was.

I felt a hand on my shoulder. I knew that the old man had gone.

"It's time to be going home now sir," the policeman said, gesturing towards the clock on the church.

The hands still indicated a time which bore no relation to the hour.... or day.

---

* This story is set near the old Dudley Station below the castle because that is how I imagined it when I heard it. The real tragedy, in which Able Seaman James Horton tried to save Clifford Albert Smith and Albert Edward Parkes, occurred in November 1923 near Dudley South Station in New Road. Since this story was written, a tribute to the dead sailor has been added to the grave of the two boys outside Top Church in Dudley.

THE COLLECTOR

She looked at her watch. Again. Yes, it was the third time in five minutes that she had had recourse to the elegant golden timepiece on her wrist. She tried to calm herself down.

Looking at her watch had two quite contradictory effects. It always reminded her of those days of long lost youth when he had given it as an act of atonement for an imagined indiscretion. It thus reminded her of how thoughtful he in fact was and, though more by way of a subtle hint than an actual reminder, of how domineering she could appear. That served to calm her down. While the watch itself had a sedative effect, the information it gave could only serve to agitate.

She could feel herself tensing up. She was going to lose control, she knew it. What came next followed an invariable pattern. Her hands fanned out, the fingers stretching to their full extent. She then traced her hands down the sides of her body from the base of her rib cage to a point just above her knees. The latter part of the exercise involved buckling into the beginnings of a crouch from which she would spring the moment her hands broke contact with her legs. In mid flight her arms would arc right up above her head and on landing would slap down by her side which signalled the start of three seconds rapid running on the spot terminated by a bitter sounding exclamation; Men!

The performance over, she would turn her energies away from the shortcomings of the male gender in general and focus on the shortcomings of one particular member of that class of objects; her man! At times she didn't know why she had married him. She could have got someone better. Someone more executive that is, better prospects. Hadn't her mother always maintained this. No prospects, below your station. On thinking this she always let a wave of guilt pass through her. Her mental recriminations would always stop there.

She felt a little better for her ritual tantrum but the release of pressure was far from absolute. There could be no doubt that the entire day had been ruined by his thoughtlessness. Man? He was more like a child. All her friends had husbands whose hobbies could be discussed dispassionately at those dreary suburban coffee mornings that Mrs Tomlinson seemed so fond of organising. In reality she hated those clucking women who were steeped in predictability. She hated them all the more because of the predictability of their husbands. They played golf, slept while watching Match of the Day, professed to be of the cognoscenti when it came to malt whisky.... but not hers, oh no, he had to be different. As a result, all the dreary women came to think of Thomas Aldridge as a dreary man. He had no hobbies, he did none of the things that their husbands did by way of relaxation. They concluded that this must be the case because the rather neurotic Mrs Aldridge never complained the way they did about their men and Mrs Aldridge was first among formidable equals when it came to complaining.

That's how the coffee group first discovered her neurosis. It was treated with fear initially; fear of the unknown that is because while they had all read about neurotics in their magazines, no one could state for certain that they had ever seen one. A woman who complains as much as Mrs Aldridge must be neurotic someone had once concluded and that conclusion had become fact. No one spoke to Mrs Aldridge for a fortnight as the psychiatric advisor to the group reported quite ably and graphically what a psychopath was capable of. Only when someone else reported that they had a neurotic in their family who wouldn't have a carving knife in the house was the possibility aired that a neurotic and a psychopath were different. It wasn't long before Mrs Aldridge was declared safe and indeed a person who required not only sympathy, but also the support of her peer group. They concluded that as Mrs Aldridge never complained about her husband's habits then it must be those very habits that were behind her neurosis. They thought it odd that a man could be so dreary as to make his wife neurotic. Surely no one could be that dull.

The discovery that Mr Aldridge left his house near Warley Woods at nine o'clock most Sunday mornings and always returned at twelve fifteen, invariably grinning like the cat who has just had the cream, altered entirely the nature of the speculation. It was obvious that he was having an affair. It was obvious after following him on three consecutive Sunday mornings to different houses that he was either having several affairs or a different woman every week. Poor Mrs Aldridge.

When he pulled onto the drive as usual that Sunday, twelve fifteen precisely and his standard broad grin, the two spies drove away armed with total disgust for that wretch of a man. Mrs Aldridge would be offered the support of the whole group without reservation.

Sunday dinner was always at one o'clock in the Aldridge household and she didn't mind in the least him visiting other collectors on Sunday mornings provided he was back by quarter to. That he was always back half an hour before this didn't prevent her from lapsing into a state of great agitation.

"I'm home," he always announced, and on entering the lounge he would kiss her delicately proffered cheek as she stood next to the doorway. She would then put the vegetables on to boil and begin to unwind. She knew that her anxiety was entirely of her own making. From what she had heard from the other women she was indeed very lucky to have such a

45

man. Their husbands would go out drinking at Sunday lunch time and wouldn't be seen again until mid afternoon and then in alcoholic insensibility, completely soused. At least her Thomas didn't drink. She realised that she should be thankful and that she shouldn't begrudge him his only hobby. If only it was a hobby of which she could be proud, or, at least, not ashamed. But collecting toy cars! How on earth could she admit to her husband's childlike preoccupation with the minutiae of miniature vehicles. How could any self-respecting woman admit such a quirk in her husband. She didn't know so she never made the admission.

He had been so upset when the results of the tests came through. They both had been, naturally. No couple wishes to be told that they can't have children. No woman wants to be told that she is barren but all those years ago it happened to Mrs Aldridge. And that was the word the doctor had used, a cruel word, barren. Despite her total flappability in most other departments her coping mechanisms on this score were astounding. It always amazed Mrs Aldridge that she was infertile yet she was the strong one. However, she had never thought or dreamt of having children and looked back on this as her unconscious telling her that her life would be childless. She wasn't surprised when she was told for once and for all; she already knew.

The news wrecked Thomas and he withdrew into himself at first. The withdrawal was replaced by anger, the anger of one who feels persecuted and unable to understand the reason behind the persecution. The doctor also told Mrs Aldridge that the wives of infertile men often went of in search of ripe seed. No comfort in any case, but their roles were quite the opposite. That didn't stop her from transforming the idea to her own situation so in this phase she felt that at any time she could lose him to another woman. Any fertile woman was a threat. She suspiciously eyed the friends they had round to dinner. It got to the stage where the other woman only had to speak to him to send Mrs Aldridge into the palpitations of severe insecurity. That an affectionate husband was in attendance and that polite conversation was supposed to be part and parcel of a dinner party escaped Mrs Aldridge in the depths of her paranoia. She was never actually overtly rude to her guests but people began to decline even the invitations of Thomas with whom they sympathised greatly. Mrs Aldridge herself had long since ceased to invite people around as she could not stand other threatening females in her house. At first Thomas's continued invitations to their friends annoyed her intensely but their loyalty to him had its limits and one by one they gave the couple up. Mrs Aldridge assumed that her anger had been responsible for the eventual end of their social life, which of course it had, but friendship was one thing that Thomas wouldn't sacrifice even for her. He himself put the change in attitude down to him recently being made foreman at the chemical plant at which he worked. It meant more responsibility obviously, but it also meant that his take-home pay dropped because he was no longer entitled to the productivity bonuses that the men on the shop floor had come to take for granted. The men thought anyone who took the foreman's job was a fool because of the effect it had on the pay packet. Thomas always looked upon bonuses as bonuses however, so, that the increase in basic pay didn't make up for the loss of the bonus didn't matter. His real pay had gone up and he had moved one step up the ladder. His wife supported his change of status, looking at it as the first of inevitably more promotions which would lead to undisputed financial as well as social advancement. He wrote the loss of friends off as a further price that had to be paid for his changed status. That none of his social acquaintances came from his workplace didn't enter into the equation. Neither did the fact that the friends he had lost were mostly managers already anyway.

They had all known him from school days when it became obvious early on that his passing to the local grammar school had either been due to one day of complete inspiration or a fluke. But he was a jovial, rotund chap a few inches shorter than his peers, in no way a threat to anyone's pretences and thus immensely likeable. In the fifth form, when the opposite sex had become important, he had lost his puppy fat and found that he had what his academic superiors hadn't; a very accomplished style of chat with the girls. It wasn't long before it became more apparent that he didn't require a line in chat at all as the girls seemed to follow him in droves anyway. He was a young man to befriend if one lacked the confidence or the patter. He couldn't cope with them all and a mythology grew as to how many he did in fact cope with. He left school at the end of the fifth while the others went on to sixth form and then university. But they remained close friends. They were surprised when, after a lightening courtship, Thomas married an intense girl two years his senior. It seemed a case of the mighty having fallen, Irene Compton didn't seem his type at all. That Irene Compton was sexually unlike anything Thomas had ever encountered before would remain unknown to them. That that was the reason behind him marrying her would always remain unknown to Irene.

That Thomas had no doubt "had" all of the women of whom she was now so suspicious in the wild days of his youth added to her condition. It also intensified her evening performances to a fever pitch. Thomas didn't mind so much losing his friends as his wife exhausted him night after night. Her thinking was that she would satisfy him so well that he wouldn't want another woman. He had never told her that she was in a league of her own and that the increased tempo made him too tired for all the women he didn't want anyway.

It was in this stage of the relationship that he forgot about it being a permanently childless one. The new and unexpected promotion, the desertion by his friends and his wife's ministrations all helped in this process. The latter served to remind him that he was getting old, or rather allowed him to convince himself that he was a lot older than he actually was.

He looked at himself in the mirror one weekend and was horrified that the flesh appeared to be dropping off him. Weekends were bad, terrible in fact. There was nothing else for them to do once the shopping was in. The shock of his drawn features staring back at him in the mirror convinced him that he would have to take action before he was whittled down to nothing.

The answer came to him instantaneously. A hobby. He would find a hobby to occupy his time at weekends. Which hobby to take up came to him with equal ease due to a newspaper article which had taken him by surprise. He had read that someone had sold a collection of Dinkey Toys for over five hundred pounds. This made him wonder whether the Dinkey Toys he had left at his parents house when he got married were worth anything. His aunts and uncles made a religion out of buying him Dinkey Toys at Christmas and birthdays until he was well into his teens. The sad part about it at the time was that he wasn't in the least bit interested in toy motor vehicles. In fact many of these toys had remained in their boxes from the day that they had been packed. He had looked into the possibility that he too might be sitting on a substantial amount of money though he doubted that he could be the possessor of such luck. He was surprised to find that there were magazines and a nationwide network of collectors who met regularly for the purpose of sales and exchanges. From one of the magazines he was astounded when he calculated that the Dinkeys at his parents house, most of which were in mint condition, were worth between eight and nine hundred pounds. He resolved to keep them as an investment as he could see no reason why the bottom should drop out of the toy car market. He wasn't after all in the least bit interested in toy cars.

But that was before he had decided that he needed a hobby. Why, he already had one. He already had a collection to be proud of. In an instant he was a collector of toy cars and lorries.

Over the years his collection grew and grew until it was worth in excess of two thousand pounds. He had it insured. He tended it with the loving care a father might show for his son. Mrs Aldridge was convinced the collection had become a substitute for a son and for that reason she bore his strange hobby in silence and isolation.

Thomas had returned that week with an absolute gem at a knockdown price. He took it upstairs to the spare bedroom which housed his collection.

He locked himself in and rearranged everything so that the new item had pride of place at the centre of the collection. Every sunday he used his half hour before lunch to be alone with his collection. It was a ritual, his wife was always out of harms way in the kitchen. At quarter to one he went downstairs for his lunch. Later on in the afternoon his wife would lock him in the main bedroom.

The following week at the coffee morning Mrs Aldridge could detect a change in atmosphere without being able to define at first what it was. Without being paranoid she began to feel that they were all looking at her. She didn't feel paranoid because they were caring looks of a guardian angel rather than the malicious daggers stared by the malcontent. And when people spoke the tones were kind, almost syrupy.

Mrs Aldridge was in the kitchen as it was her turn to be the guardian of the kettle. Having a few minutes to herself, she began to ponder the apparent change in attitude. Was it real or imagined? Was it directed at her? If so why was it directed at her?

The two women who had spent the last four Sundays following Thomas to his trysts stealthily entered the kitchen. Mrs Aldridge was unaware of their presence and gave a start when she eventually saw them hovering at the extremity of her sideways vision. She turned to face the two women whose countenances bore strange looks of understanding. She looked at them questioningly. Being more or less confronted, the two women hesitated in their task. Mrs Aldridge's gaze became more imploring. One of the women finally got out, mouthing the words moreso than saying them, "It's alright dear, we know."

Mrs Aldridge watched the mouth spell out its message but she was never any good with that form of communication which was generally reserved for relating female operations in male company. The sounds were nowhere near as loud as a whisper so Mrs Aldridge stared blankly at the women unaware of what exactly was going on. A sharp jolt of anxiety made her realise that whatever it was, it was of utmost importance.

The second woman decided not to stand on ceremony and blurted out quite clearly, "We know!"

Mrs Aldridge was rigid. She was now aware that they knew, that in all probability they all knew and that that was the reason behind their kind smiles and sincere tones. Mrs Aldridge was at once troubled. What did they know? In the dark depths of her mind lurked the thought that it might be about Thomas, they might know about Thomas. That was an impossibility however as there was nothing that could betray that secret; nothing had been said, nothing had been done. That particular secret was surely as safe as the Crown Jewels. It couldn't be that, so what was it that the ladies of the coffee morning knew that could be of such importance that they felt obliged to tell her of it in so strange a manner. She looked puzzled.

The woman read the question on Mrs Aldridge's face and added by way of explanation, "About your husband."

Mrs Aldridge froze in terror. They knew that! How was it possible Her brain worked overtime quite oblivious to the comforting arms which were now around her.

She did ask "How?", which was taken to mean how did they find out and she was told that they had followed Thomas. That must have registered because it introduced all kinds of questions into her already overloaded mind. They really must have gone into it in a big way. They had gone out of their way to discover her secret and they had succeeded. They were all part of the conspiracy. She was the laughing stock. She would never be able to show her face anywhere ever again. Her husband collected toy cars and the world now knew of it. She would have embarked on a fit of uncontrollable weeping had she not fainted first.

Over the next ten minutes she drifted in and out of consciousness. There were women looking down at her, advising that she be given air while they crowded in closer for a better vantage point from which they could confirm how pale she appeared. There were mumbled expletives about Thomas plus one or two surgical amendments they thought would befit him.

Thomas could neither understand the off-hand manner of the nurses towards him when he picked up Irene at the hospital nor the cryptic invective the doctor delivered when he told him the frequency of the valium dose. He was none the wiser when he got his wife home because all she would tell him was that they knew.

Over the next few days Irene let the story out that the women at the coffee morning were now a party to the fact that he was a collector of toy motor cars. He had been completely unaware that his pride and joy, his collection, was such a great source of embarrassment to her; great enough for her to have to hide it and great enough to make her ill when it became common knowledge. Had he known he could have taken her along to meet the other collector's wives - some of the collectors were wives. He could have nipped it in the bud by showing her at the outset that it was quite a common, respectable hobby patronised by professional folk, a few M.P.s and a smattering of the gentry. In short, it was nothing to be embarrassed about at all. Knowing the mental states his wife was well capable of manufacturing for herself the response was hardly surprising once the initial misconception had been arrived at. What did surprise him was the hostility his collecting toy cars engendered among his wife's social circle. She had many callers over the week, both in person and over the telephone, and they were all hostile to Thomas to some degree. Some were just cold toward him, treating him as though he didn't exist; some were mildly rude and others very rude. That collecting toy cars warranted castration was a thought that alarmed Thomas when it was first put to him by one of the more extreme ladies of the coffee morning. She maintained that not only should that be his lot for his Sunday morning activities, but that castration should be the lot of all who indulged in that sort of thing. Thomas thought better of asking whether female collectors were to have their ovaries removed of their Fallopian tubes sewn up or indeed, something quite unimaginable sutured. His pondering aloud how they would use the lavatory gave one of the extremists the impression that they hadn't listened to a word she had said which prompted her to slap him sharply across the face. The naked aggression compounded Mrs Aldridge's misery, she had no idea of the depth of feelings collecting toy cars aroused in the general population. She burst into tears and Thomas was slapped again on the other cheek.

It took many months to persuade Irene that collecting toy cars was innocuous and that it was indeed quite respectable. The first part of the process involved persuading her that those women from the coffee mornings were unrepresentative if not insane. The women themselves looked upon the absence of Mrs Aldridge from their gatherings as the actions of a woman diligently trying to mend a broken marriage. No praise could be high enough for their long-suffering absent friend. For her part, Mrs Aldridge avoided all of the women as though they carried a deadly contagion for fear of renewed embarrassment.

By the time she accidentally encountered one of the ladies at a bus stop, her attitude had altered completely from her days of ignorance. Thomas had painstakingly educated her into the ways of a collector. She now accompanied him to meetings and on Sunday morning purchases. The woman concerned was loathe to ask how things were between her and Thomas but eventually, after much circumlocution, managed to put the question as tactlessly as was her wont. Mrs Aldridge didn't bat an eyelid when the subject was broached. She was like a cured alcoholic, unafraid to speak of her former illness.

"Oh, he still does it", she stated with a confidence which staggered the recipient of the information. She was at once filled with admiration for the woman who was able to come to terms so bravely with the situation of having so incorrigible a philanderer as a husband. Her admiration was in no measure as great as the horror she experienced when Mrs Aldridge calmly stated that she went to watch her husband every week. Mrs Aldridge couldn't understand why someone should stand at a bus-stop for so long and then suddenly decide to run home without so much as a goodbye. Perhaps Thomas had been right; they were all mad.

The Aldridges became known as a team in collecting circles and were as well liked as Thomas had been when he had been on his own. Their collection became quite famous; the envy of the region. Mrs Aldridge however still referred to it as his collection and still had bouts of neurosis. Her big doubt was whether he loved her or his collection, but she reconciled herself to the fact that that was something no wife would ever know, be it of her husband's collection, his fishing or his football team.

The accident was a very bad one. It came just at the time when there was talk of Thomas joining the under-management, the next step up the ladder. All those aspirations paled into insignificance as he struggled through, and eventually won, a protracted battle to remain alive. The convalescent period stretched into its second year and without really knowing how it happened, the Aldridge household was confronted with some unpayable bills. Confused and without a single idea of what to do about the situation, the final demands started to arrive.

Irene thought of selling her watch but that wouldn't have covered any one of the bills let alone the full half dozen. She was out trying to secure a loan from the bank when the gentleman called. He left with half of the collection in exchange for a substantial amount in cash.

Mrs Aldridge returned without having managed to secure a loan. The receipts for the bills were on the table paid in full. She cried when she saw the room with the collection decimated.

Thomas smiled. "I knew I'd show you one day that it wasn't a waste of time."

STREET SCENE

Hall Street had been narrow. Little shops, with wares hanging in the dirty breeze. The ironmongers and butchers, the greengrocers. Poultry and vegetables catching the blackness of the air. Doubtless knives and axes hung too but, I was told, it was the food which stuck in the craw of William Joyce. Lord Haw Haw. Germany called Dudley dirty, unhygenic. Horrible town, horrible people. The dirty shops and pubs of Hall Street would be bombed flat by the Third Reich.

In the same broadcast, apparently, Joyce professed an intimate knowledge of the area. The picturesque Staffordshire village of Kinver had, he informed listeners, briefly been his home though I could find no reference of it in a biography. Kinver, clean and beautiful. The village and people would survive and prosper under the new order. It was the squat ugliness that the Arian regime would remove. Highly commendable in many respects and highly amusing in many others. There was a war on and outside Kinver was a huge ammunition dump beneath the hills. That Hitler wasn't going to bomb our munitions dump must have been a bit of a laugh and that none of his bombs ever came remotely close to hitting, let alone levelling, the loathed Hall Street must have been a bigger one.

Hall Street remained unchanged through the austere post war years. In the early sixties when there was work and money about the shop fronts were no different to those depicted in the postcards of the twenties. It was the people walking past them who had changed. The teenage revolution was in full swing. The Beatles were idolised by the new generation and feared by the old. Paul married Jane and the Beatles were their band. Every Beatles song was their song.

Hall Street was closed. The days of the pedestrian precinct were upon the nation, as new and exciting as the music..... or as terrifying. Mosaic walls, flower beds and benches, trees, shop fronts all glass psychedelic colouring, brightness, spaciousness, glass. Wares kept clean behind glass and a Clean Air Act kept the sky visibly cleaner. There were more trees in Dudley now.

Churchill Precinct it was called. Was the war fought to ascertain who should be responsible for the demolition of Hall Street. The British won, the British tore down their own streets and built up new ones. Churchill. The victor. His precinct.

Twenty years after opening the precinct still stood. The arty glass mosaic no longer in one piece. The wooden sculpture across the footbridge no longer offensive. The new Churchill in power. The floor so slippy that a little rain made walking precarious. Closing down sales. Discount stores.

Cheap goods from the far east. The free market economy in full swing. There had been a disproportionate number of butchers and shoe shops. Five of each to begin with, now there was only one. Boutiques and tailors had come and gone. Cafés gone. The pub gone. The Post Office gone. Buskers had come and little else beside. Street artists were a sign of the free market economy.

Next to one of the central display cases stood a young man with an acoustic guitar, a twinkle in someone's eye when the precinct had been built. The first bloom of youth on his cheeks, a dirty blue bandana round his neck and a trilby hat perched high on a tangled head of hair. The leather jacket and corduroy trousers completed a picture of dishevelment and poverty. The holes in the trainers and dirty socks were a give away. The sturdy guitar case had a light covering of coins of low denomination.

He had a good voice that bellowed above the brisk strumming. It was a Beatles medley. A woman stood just to one side of the display case. Her clothes were nondescript. She cut no ice with the surroundings. Her head was bowed and she was crying. The masses moved past her without noticing, without caring. Jane had lost Paul and an uncomfortable youth sang their songs to an indifferent audience. Their indifference made her cry all the more. She fumbled about in her purse and threw a five pound note into the guitar case and wandered home.

The busker stopped shortly afterwards. That old woman had been hanging around all day. Who'd have thought a fiver though. Thank God somebody listened, thank God somebody cared. He packed up and went home.

A dirty breeze still blew at the wares. The glass shop fronts prevented the fumes from reaching anything but the lungs of the pedestrians. An acid rain washed the slippery tiles. There were fewer trees in Kinver these days.

THE EFFRONTERY

Outside the streets were full and the air still. Inside the Lounge Bar of *The Red Lion* there was still a sense of coolness as the Xpelair coped with the efforts of the few smokers at air pollution. Little of the morning sunshine filtered through the windows. It was a corner pub; on one side was a narrow street and the other faced completely the wrong way to catch any sun. The exterior had a strangely Germanic aspect; ornate turrets, a clock tower. It was a quaintly gothic scene straight out of a 1930s spoof horror movie. Such a facade required no sun. The inside had of course been refurbished long since. Gone were the etched lead-glass mirrors and ornate rose-wood bars. In its place the drab uniform functionalism of the 1970s. Formica bar top, red lighting and a lot of plastic. A juke box hammered out some heavy metal. It was a bikers pub.

Karl Houseman was sweating profusely. Nervously he lit up a cigarette. He brushed his tangled hair out of his eyes and took another swig of cider. Even the beer in there was plastic so he drank cider. What else he was doing in there he could not imagine but drinking off a Saturday morning hangover had to start somewhere.

There were some bikers in. Karl knew a lot of them, had known them for years in fact. As individuals he could get on with most of them. He even liked one or two of them but was wary of the lunatic fringe who solved problems by means of violence. He could say the same about any set of people with a group identity. With the bikers however, when it came to politics he was inclined to label them uniformly as fascists in spirit.

More bikers came in and their talk was of politics. Karl was disinclined to stay and listen to the moronic ramblings of a bunch of fascists. There was a friendly exchange as Karl left on finishing his drink. They knew why the communist was leaving. Karl was deemed a sound bloke except for his politics.

He picked his way through the shoppers, his hangover far from cured. His mind kept glancing back to the night before. Through not being able to stomach the fascists he was out on the street and yet in the neighbouring town the real fascists were staging a march through the shopping centre that very morning. There had been a lot of publicity locally about the British Front Party marching; protests from traders and trade unionists, councillors and clergy. The police chiefs ummed and arred and finally O.K.'d the proceedings. The dispossessed bachelors of the far and soft left had debated it in full the night before. The big marches of the late '70s were called to mind which attracted huge counter demonstrations which necessitated a large police presence and, more often than not, ended in bloodshed. Those were different days, the days of consensus when it was a hard job trying to differentiate between the rightish Labour Party and a comparatively leftish Tory Party. There was no S.D.P., the Liberals had been in decline for over half a century and were only just starting to re-emerge. The fascists of Britain were organised. By the time of the '79 election they were ready to contest in excess of 300 constituencies. They claimed that they were becoming Britain's third political force. The two party system was beginning to look shaky and with an economic crisis on the horizon who knew. The far left used the words of Hitler to drum up support for opposing the tide. "The only way we could of been stopped was to have kicked us off the streets in our early days." Or words to that effect. The remit of the hard left was to physically stop the fascists whenever and wherever they tried to march. The broad spectrum Anti Nazi League grew out of the left's opposition and the public's concern. Karl thought it was probably the greatest service the far left ever paid the nation when it succeeded in halting the fascist tide. They weren't free to march ....

Ah but that was then. The times changed, the fascists fragmented and faded. The Alliance formed the third choice in British politics while Thatcher and her crew flung the country to the right. Whoever said it the night before was right, the fascists were no longer a threat, demonstrating against a gang of misguided skinheads was a futile gesture when viewed against those who held power in Whitehall.

Those who wanted to demonstrate used the same arguments of the previous decade and marched while those who didn't just said Thatcher or Tebbitt and stayed at home. Karl was more inclined toward the former argument than the latter but had forgotten all about it until just now. It was true that the British Front Party no longer rankled him either. Not quite sure whether it was out of need to immerse himself in the font of traditional British liberalism or that he was just plain thirsty, he headed for the only overtly gay establishment in town, *The Long Bar*. Maybe it was both. With all the brain space he'd devoted to fascists real and imagined he needed reassurance that he, if not the rest of the country, was tolerant of others..... and he still needed a drink or two to relieve his hangover.

The Long Bar was on the High Street and its name was as good a description as most would give it. A lot of money had been spent in moving the bar from one side of the room to the other. There wasn't a lot else the designers could do with a glorified corridor but someone must have thought it worth the effort. The new bar had a ceramic surface, green and brown patterned tiles matching the mosaiced glass lamp shades. The lighting was as soft as the music and a bevy of continental lager bottles filled the modern glass fronted refrigerator. Two pretty contoured girls not long out of school served suggestively a clientele who were basically disinterested in what they had to offer while the landlady held court at a stool by the bar. A waitress in a pink check smock scurried in and out of the kitchen with chili con carnes and shepherds pies, her menu both exotic and basic.

There were a few elderly shoppers in eating lunch as they had done for years. Near the door a young couple were kissing between sips of their drinks. The rest of the room was sparsely filled with young men. Some were drinking alone, reading papers, one young man read a science fiction book. Others were talking in small groups. Karl blended into the relaxed atmosphere almost unnoticed. He stood alone at the bar appreciating the mood of the establishment.

He had been there about ten minutes when they made their entrance. Some people had come and some had gone but the atmosphere had remained relaxed. There were six of them. The one at the front seemed to be the leader, the others filed behind. They were talking loudly about not backing away from a fight and what a shambles it had been.

The peace was shattered. The elderly clientele looked on uneasily, distrustful of the youth of the day when they were so loud. The young man put down his book and the chatter ceased. The mob had made their entrance. The young bar staff stood agape, unsure of what to do. The uneasiness of the elderly had pervaded the entire room.

The six lads were well built, clipped T shirts displayed their muscular physiques. Heavy booted feet displayed their potential aggression. They were members of the British Front Party. Their march had been something of a washout with very few turning up. They had been angry at the apparent ineptitude of their leaders and needed to prove something to themselves. They exuded an aura of volatility and unpredictability.

Approaching the bar near Karl the leader called for six pints of lager. The bar staff were silent, it was their play.

With immaculate timing the landlady had peeled away from the bar and was between the leader and his men. "All eighteen are we?" she delivered in a steady voice with a firm gaze directed at the leader. She added the words "lads" very pointedly.

The leader stood alone and almost spat back his yes, isolated and unconvincing. "Are we sure?" the land lady went on, directing her gaze at the men. They were broken. No one would own to being eighteen except for the leader.

The order changed to one pint of lager and five cokes, all of which were consumed with great rapidity, the exit being no where near as stage managed as the entrance. They left unnoticed.

Karl mused about the state of organised fascism and was quite glad he hadn't got up to march against the likes of those youths. With his second drink inside him his head felt a lot better so he decided to walk on down to *The Light* were he might get a report on the counter demonstration.

On his way out he heard one of the young men saying "Yes, but the real fascists are in Whitehall." He suddenly felt no better after all.

A HEN PARTY

Thursday night was stag night. Or hen night depending on your gender. And of course depending on you either getting married at the weekend or being an intimate of someone getting married at the weekend.

John was neither getting married at the weekend nor knew anyone who was getting married at the weekend. Leastways, if he did then they hadn't let him in on the secret. He had just finished a late shift and had decided on a quick beer in *The Light*, the town centre pub he called his local. He was a latent homosexual. He didn't go out with women but he didn't go out with men exactly either. He liked the company in the Light, mostly radicals and socialists, mostly men, one or two of them practising gays. There were one or two feminists too.

John liked mixing with people who were intelligent and aware but what troubled him was that there seemed to go with that state an assumption that the entire population was equally intelligent and aware. Just how certain newspapers sold so well or why certain television programmes were so popular was, in that case, beyond him. There was such a thing as vulgarity, all the great writers of the past constantly referred to it so it must exist even in the eyes of his intelligent and aware peer group. Being of an intelligent and aware peer group however he wasn't exposed to much, if any, vulgarity at all. He often wondered if he was missing out on life.

He hadn't noticed a bus outside but it was obvious on entering the lounge bar that a bus load was in fact in. Someone was obviously getting married on Saturday and this particular party of hens were hell bent on having a good time. From their thick accents John could tell that they were working class. Or was it that they were seemingly enjoying themselves too much to be middle class.

He bought his drink in the nick of time before ten ladies of various ages shapes and sizes charged to the bar. One of them bumped into him by accident. Without thinking about it he had apologised in a sincere tone which was the only reason the woman turned round and looked at him. After a few seconds thought he smiled.

John positioned himself near to his socialist friends who were sitting at a table in the corner. There were no spare seats so he remained standing. At the next table two feminists chuntered on about sexual harassment at work. They were too engrossed in their conversation to be aware of what was going on around them. They at least looked like part of the scenery.

The rest of the room was taken up by revellers. Some of them were standing, others were sitting. John couldn't help but be struck by the detached appearance of the group at the edge of which he was standing. They looked out of place in the scene of proletarian revelry. Some looked aloof, others looked a little disgusted by the noisy incursion into their world of intelligent awareness.

Another round of drinks in and the bar was again free. The woman who had bumped into John had returned to her friend with a drink, one of many through the course of the evening by the look of her. Her friend was a corpulent rosy faced woman with auburn hair and a huge bust. She wore a black dress, the short sleeves of which revealed thick arms, muscular through factory work. Her legs were sturdy and her buttocks ample. The woman who had made bodily contact with John now made eye contact. She was blonde, far more petite than her friend and her face was heavily made up. She smiled once she had been noticed and whispered to her friend. They laughed raucously. Two of the socialists looked up and tutted loudly.

The whole gang were going on to some night club afterwards. The chatter was innuendo-ridden with much reference to the penis. Last orders came and went. John was disinterested in the socialists' conversation and the feminists were too wrapped up to admit him into their proceedings and besides, he was a man. John wondered whether men were ever sexually harassed. He stared at the two feminists who were happily condemning an entire gender. This seemed little different, to John, than condemning an entire race though he felt sure that these particular two women were politically sound.

The forty or so women began to drink up and head on to their night club. John had no doubt that, for some of them, the references to penises would be a reality before very many hours elapsed. The two feminists continued to argue for their gender oblivious that forty or so fully paid-up members of it were about to leave. John wondered whether the feminists were aware of ordinary women at all.

The petite blonde brushed past John again, this time quite deliberately. She turned and smiled and apologised sarcastically. Her corpulent friend followed but instead of walking past John, turned and gave him a less than gentle squeeze of his testicles and penis. John winced in pain and whelped a bit like a dog. The two feminists looked up and stared at John malevolently. The two women scurried away laughing loudly, they were having a good time. The socialists looked at the clock. Peace at last but the bar was shut, so their faces still displayed the self-righteous disgust which had been their feature for the evening.

John went home. It had been a long time since a woman had touched him privately. He had quite enjoyed the experience. He half toyed with the idea of following the women to the night club but he had to be up in the morning before day break for the early shift. Besides, he wasn't used to vulgarity. He would be back in *The Light* the following evening for more intelligent awareness.

FIGHT NIGHT

The *Army & Navy Bar* was fuller than he had ever seen it. Men in shirt sleeves tried to keep cool by avoiding bodily contact. Maintaining ones personal space seemed the prime concern on this sultry evening. Some wives sat disconsolately on the bench seats by the wall watching the glamourous old girl with the blue tinted hair rattle change into the gambling machine as her cigarette dropped ash lazily to the floor.

Someone said something about the march in Brierley Hill. Ray thought twice about his answer. The *Army & Navy Bar* might have been one of the friendliest in town but it was also the most overtly right wing. He mumbled something and got away with it. He wasn't sure which side he was viewed to be on. At any rate Raymond Bragg soon learned that the National Front march had been a fiasco. Only eighty had turned up due to a breakdown in communications and a rumour that it had been cancelled at the last minute. Two hundred on the counter demonstration including eighteen Labour councillors. It all sounded good but it was nothing compared to the '70s. There would have been a lot of police too, Ray thought.

He was late. He was to have seen Irene but she was unwell and holed up in the Yuppie quarter of Birmingham. Where she belonged Ray mused but it was too hot for vitriol and what were all those people doing out. Maybe it was the sun, or maybe it was the fact that it was Easter Saturday. Why stay indoors glued to a television screen pumping out American drivel.

Ray was soon enlightened. "There's that fight on in a minute" he heard someone say. Hunnigan was defending his world title. Ray wasn't sure what weight or against whom he was fighting but he vaguely remembered something from somewhere about a title defence.

The spectacle soon started for Ray. The men watching he fight rather than the fight itself. They were all engrossed in it, fists clenched, jaws set, bobbing and weaving with the action in the ring. A fist would sometimes rise up slowly above the waist in frustration at an opportunity missed by one of the fighters. Between rounds the men would take out bets or alter bets about which round would see it finished.

There was no colour bar in the *Army & Navy Bar* but neither were there any blacks. The men were all regulars from neighbourhood pubs which had been "taken over" by the "darkies". *The Laughing Cavalier* - "darkies pub". *The Tree* - "darkies pub". The "darkies" had apparently spoilt these establishments though no one was likely to venture how. The *Army & Navy Bar* was a sanctuary - "no darkies in there." Safe from the presence of "darkies" the men drank, joked and bet while they watched the two black men on the screen.

Ray found himself at the bar just before closing time which was just after the fight had spun out to a ten round draw. Sally was serving. A good looking blonde girl with a striking figure and suggestive eyes. She was married but would flirt overtly with the men. Nothing physical, nothing in it, she had a knack of making the men feel welcome, especially the lonely men. The flash of the eyes and the puckering of the lips, the smiles and the winks, the very inviting body language. She was good at her job and gave those with nothing something to dream of.

She was right in front of Ray when it happened with just the bar between them. The steward was behind the bar and Ray saw the hand rise up. He thought it would playfully press her breast but instead a nipple bulged out in Ray's direction projected by the harsh pressure of the stewards squeeze. Sally squealed softly, suggesting that such treatment was commonplace. She broke from his grip and turned in embarrassment. The steward grinned heartily at an expressionless Ray. A red faced Sally fumbled change into his hand, her eyes averted.

Ray made his way back to his seat from the bar through the men who were guffawing at the pawing of a tit. It had been more entertaining than those two "darkies" on the television. It was some time before Sally's complexion returned to its normal colour. All the winks and smiles were going the other way now. Ray was learning about the *Army & Navy Bar*. There were unwritten laws about women too.

SNOWSTORM

It was bitterly cold for the end of March, I thought, as an icy blast of wind propelled me in a direction in which I did not want to go. Still, that hill *was* a bit exposed. To the north and east the Midlands Plain arced way below; the factories of the Black Country and the expanding skyline of Birmingham. Nothing at that height to the east until the Ural Mountains way over in Russia some folk said. I didn't know about that but it did seem a bit Siberian at times up there and when the winds blew they blew with a vengeance. Sometimes in a storm I felt like running round the estate shouting "Batten down the hatches me hearties!" The nautical references had been induced into my life by the person in the flat upstairs, whom I never saw, who made the most peculiar noises on my ceiling. It was as though he had only one leg and his wooden stump would bang the floor, the sound resonating through my own flat. The only time I knew him to be quiet was one afternoon of a Bank Holiday when the film "Moby Dick" was being shown on television. It confirmed my theory as I imagined him to be sat in hushed reverence watching his hero Captain Ahab.

The sky was grey but a diffuse sunlight lit the landscape clear to the horizon. To the south and west the gently rolling hills of Worcestershire and Shropshire unfolded. I could see the Clee Hills some thirty miles off on the horizon. No snow about. It was certainly cold enough but there was none in the air. Besides, the country had had its snow for the year. Back in January the town had been brought to a standstill within the space of a few hours by a heavy afternoon fall. It had made me think of what the hill had been like in Saxon times. Would they have holed-up on the leeside with camp fires roaring, secure in the knowledge that the Danes wouldn't send raiding parties out in bad weather? Would they have cracked out the strong winter brew? Would they have listened to the visiting bard recite the latest epic, "Beowulf Two", or would it have been a repeat of one of those wretched Icelandic sagas? Snow was good for the imagination.

My car stood alone in one of the parking bays. As I approached it my heart sank. There could be no mistake that the rear offside tyre was as flat as a pancake. My first thought was vandals, there had been a spate of incidents recently in which cars had been damaged. I muttered expletives as I set about changing the wheel.

The damage had been done by a three-inch nail so it wasn't vandals after all. The tyre would need repair but it wouldn't be a write-off, I thought as I put on the spare. That place down the east side of the hill towards the motorway was good. They would be able to do the job quickly enough for me to still be in time for work.

Within five minutes I was turning left past the iron gates onto the private road. There was a modern bungalow on the right facing the main road, but a hundred yards behind it, hidden by a bend in the track, was the tyre place; a corrugated-iron structure, a real ramshackle affair. The tyre place dealt in cut-price tyres which they bought in bulk from wrecks and write-offs.

Signs displaying "Dunlop", "Goodyear", "Firestone", "Ferodo", littered the walls. The smell of rubber filled the air. On the way up the track I could have sworn I saw a few snow flakes alight on the windscreen before melting into droplets. I could see the fire roaring in the old stove inside. It looked warm and inviting as indeed, an angry snow cloud loomed overhead.

The foreman came across the yard to me as I got the flat tyre out of the boot. A sleek BMW 5-series was parked right next to the closed wall of the workshop. The owner was looking for a new set of wide-wheeled tyres, a great expense even there. A Sierra with low profiles sat next to the fence, no cheap job either. Weeds pushed their way through the railings. One of the men rolled the flat through the open front of the workshop. The snow came swirling down, sticking to hair and clothes, brushing the ground with greyness.

The tyre place was out on its own in a field. It couldn't really be seen from anywhere and nothing in particular could be seen from it save the tangled weeds on the expanse of waste ground beyond the railings. The snow fell heavily. The foreman called me over to wait in the warm while one of the men saw to my tyre.

In the warmth of the workshop I brushed the snow from my coat and gazed out at the blizzard. I was enchanted by the isolation. A little garage, a tyre place, seemingly out in the middle of nowhere. It was the easiest thing in the world to forget that it was in the middle of a vast conurbation and I did so. I imagined being on a lonesome highway somewhere in the United States, hours drive away from the nearest town. A thrill of being stranded captured my senses.

Outside it had gone as dark as a winter dusk in which the lights seem to glow all the more. There were three pneumatic tyre-changing machines in the workshop, a few troughs filled with water to test for leaks, and high-pressure air lines hung down at convenient points.

The inside room served as an office. In there the stove threw out welcome heat. In the corner was a pile of kindling and scrap wood. The foreman took a few pieces and fed the flames.

The man had removed the tyre from the wheel and found that the nail had gone right the way through. After marking the spot he took the nail out with pliers then repaired the puncture with a wad of rubber. He changed the valve on the wheel then levered the tyre back into place after brushing the edges with grease.

A Mercedes van pulled up. An Indian got out and said something incomprehensible. The foreman laughed and the Indian laughed too. Maybe he wanted a tyre changing. The Indian pointed and laughed. The men laughed. Now they knew which one they would be alright.

The man dipped the tyre in the trough. It seemed to have sealed O.K.. I payed the foreman and rolled the wheel back through the snow to my car. It had a half inch covering and had been there only five minutes. The blizzard showed no signs of letting up. I flung the tyre into the boot and started on my way, the headlights catching the reflections of the rapid fall. At the main road I turned right. Visibility was poor and the feeling of isolation remained. I proceeded slowly until, fifty yards up the road, the blizzard ceased. A hundred yards further on and the pavements were bone dry. The sun shone quite brightly and I was back in the conurbation. When I got to work I thought about asking if anyone else had seen any snow but I shook my head and thought better of it.

THE BOY IN THE BASEMENT

The man had called it a cellar but it wasn't really a cellar, it wasn't strictly speaking underground. But then again the man didn't appear terribly cognisant as he hovered around in the brown overalls that he'd been issued with long ago and yet still didn't seem worn or faded. The building had been a town hall but the town of Wednesbury no longer existed so it now served another function in another town although it hadn't actually moved. It wasn't far from the main entrance, at street level, that the narrow steps led down to the cellar which was dark despite the white-wash. At the rear of the cellar were two huge wooden doors which opened out onto a lower street, it was a basement.

Some basements have a more active role in the life of a building but this one seemed to serve simply as the lowest common denominator, the bottom of the building to which all the useless paraphernalia of the distant past fell. Not all the contents however were completely without use, hundred upon hundred of partitions were stacked neatly to be taken out at election time. Ballot papers are soon destroyed. Long after the final election the partitions alone would stand as testimony to the existence of "democracy".

Had the final election been held twenty years before the cellar was to have been a shelter, the shelter from which the post Armageddon society of the town which now wasn't would have been run. There was much junk; maps, first aid manuals, leaflets on radiation - its effects and what to do, or what would be done, after the detonation. There were even a number of high power volumes intelligible only to those intimate with nuclear physics. The inadequacy of both shelter and guidance seemed to compound each other to the point of ridiculousness.

Ray Bastable dwelt on the ridiculousness for a time. Then on his own ridiculousness. On how he had, for the past year, been acting in such a way that looking anything other than a fool would have proved difficult. His career, his women. He'd thrown the the former away on a dream of being the new Orwell. He'd thrown most of his self respect away on the dream of a perfect love with the latter.

It had been in the basement of his friend's flat in London that the last firm foothold had been dashed from under him to leave him swimming in a seemingly never ending torrent of life in a fast forward stream. That's how it seemed, but reality was closer to an empty, purposeless, slow death with fading points of reference and an alarming sense of nausea.

What was he doing now. Driving for a living, drifting for a port. The old drive had gone. Lab working with a bit of research and a lot of routine.

Recognizably dull but interesting to others. Writing of sorts. Inspiring, uplifting, an opiate at times but with downers thrown in revolving around self doubt about ability and long solitary hours of tedium and drudgery to hammer out form. Obsequious flatterers grew on trees his pride to boost.

Zoe was an enigma, highly intelligent with a degree in biology, she hid her light beneath a bushel. She was introduced to him as an artist however and he loved her from the start. That she wanted to know who he was didn't help and misconceptions of mutual admiration grew around the sort of pub society of alternative thinkers and livers in which he had hovered precariously. Ray didn't think he lived alternatively but being out of work and having rejection slips from a number of major houses was apparently qualification, or "street cred", enough.

Zoe was attractive. Long legged, sleek, firm of bosom and pretty of face, a face which she made up in such a way that there was a hint of the oriental about her. That added to her mystery, as did her art. "Zoe has an exhibition on you know" Ray was encouraged one time. So he took himself off on a dismal January Saturday to the library in question. At once disappointed with the work, his heart tingled for the human being while his loins stirred for the woman. It wasn't art at all. It was the work of someone who liked to spend some time painting as a form of relaxation. It lacked both style and imagination though aunties and uncles would be genuinely enthusiastic. He spent ten minutes looking at the twelve or so pictures of varying states of blandness.

The following week he saw her and spoke at some length about her paintings. He wasn't going to lie about them and didn't have to because Zoe knew herself that they weren't very good. Admitting to not being an artist and never wanting to be she said it was just something she loved doing and hoped that one day she would do it well. She had been a little embarrassed on learning that Ray had been to see the display, as she called it - the alternative community had dubbed it an exhibition. All she wanted to do was maybe sell a few pictures to aunties and uncles to raise a bit of cash towards a holiday. She did sell the odd item for a fiver or a tenner depending on how big it was.

In telling her that he had never sold so much as a line of his writing, Ray cheered her visibly. He went on to say that if he didn't enjoy writing then he would stop, that he could write for the rest of his life without being published and, that he would write for the rest of his life even if he wasn't published. That admission seemed to form a bond. He said that his real ambition was to be a good writer and that his first attempts were nowhere near good enough to print despite there being enough bad writers in print. All that gave a comfortable delusion of a common direction.

They met quite frequently over the next month as a couple. Ray would be tense, almost sick, with excitement at the prospect of being with Zoe. For her part she liked seeing him - he made her laugh and there had been precious little laughter in her recent past. The relationship was tactile from the start. They exuded the aura of lovers even if the affair was one sided. They kissed with a wreckless abandon. She stimulated him with her presence, he stimulated her with his tongue, but while the petting may have suggested one thing physically, the psychological barriers she put up suggested the exact opposite. The deeper he fell in love the more she would build walls around herself for protection against having to make any decisions. As the walls got higher and higher there had to come a point where they would seem insurmountable. As the inward process went one way the outer physical process went another, never taken as far as complete discovery but always edging insatiably in that direction.

He was surprised to put it mildly when she agreed to go to London with him for the weekend. It seemed a great leap forward in many respects but always there were the mixed messages of please keep your distance on one hand and bring your body closer on the other. Closer and closer still but never *that* close.

It was a conscious decision he took to tell her. It wasn't blurted out on the spur of the moment though it may have seemed that way to her. Those walls seemed to him to be getting a little too high, a little too close to the point of no return. It was better to have loved and lost than not to have loved at all he told himself. He told her he loved her and then watched as the walls became forever insurmountable. Ray knew from the moment the words had left his lips that they would never be, could never be. They then kissed passionately and petted furiously. Before he went home that night Zoe told him she was very fond of him. She was very fond of him and yes, she would still go to London.

It was a surprise when they got there. Ray's friend had to go up north so they had the use of his basement flat right through till Sunday. As soon as he set out Zoe and Ray threw themselves together but stopped short, panting, wanting to be lovers but scared of the consequences. She needed time, he needed her. He went for a walk. He needed time too. Ray bought a box of Turkish Delight while out and apologised for his urgency when he got back. They kissed again, this time without passion. Zoe busied herself and got ready for the theatre while he watched low budget sci-fi on the T.V. Nearly ready and raring to go up the West End she scolded him for not getting ready and watching rubbish. He watched in silence and wondered why he loved her as he made ready to leave. Ray's feelings would not leave him however and it was with pride that he took her out into the excitement of the winter capital.

Two people who cared for their friends and about their world. Two people lost and bewildered at their ineffectuality at being unable to put anything about their own lives straight let alone the lives of anyone else. Zoe liked Ray, his company, but couldn't understand why he loved her so intensely. She constantly voiced her low opinion of herself and he constantly made efforts to instill some self confidence in her. Zoe would have let herself go and been Ray's lover had love not been involved. Ray loved her and couldn't understand why the relationship was going both forwards and backwards at an almost equal velocity. He was asking for virtually nothing from her and getting mixed messages back. Your company and fun yes. Your knowledge of the world yes. Your love no. Your sexual advances yes, up to a point. Your affection no.

Funnily enough Ray had never contemplated bed or sex with Zoe even though they were away for the weekend. But once alone an animal fury was unleashed. He felt empty and unfulfilled at the afternoons events but glad that she clung to him in the chill night as they walked briskly to the tube. Zoe was afraid of losing him in the vast cosmopolitan wastes with trains coming and going and people to-ing and fro-ing. She needed him. Ray was au fait with the world, confident unperturbed by the apparent complexities of getting from A to B. Zoe was lost. Their different lives showed out all the way to the theatre.

The play itself proved well worth the trip, well acted, well directed, a good set and a moving tale but Ray couldn't help a feeling of sliding somewhere away from his present situation. Zoe jumped and gripped his arm tightly when the gun went off towards the end of the performance. It served only to jar him out of his slide momentarily. He took her to a small Italian restaurant afterwards but he couldn't eat. He was grim and taciturn. She did ask him why but he didn't say. He wasn't sure what was coming, that much he hadn't yet formulated. Ray ended up saying that he was always quiet, a casual excuse that was apparently accepted.

Back at the flat Zoe thanked him for a wonderful evening and kissed him on the cheek before going to bed. Ray remained motionless. There could be no more sexual teasing from either of them. She went straight to sleep while a wall away he watched video after video, drank coffee after coffee till there was none left in the jar. Sleep wouldn't come with his mind and body so restless. He dwelt on the walls people put up to protect themselves. He had failed to scale the wall around Zoe and now in admission of defeat he was building a wall around himself which she would find it difficult to scale but scale it she would have to in order to maintain the fun relationship. Fun. He laughed. How could there be fun now? He realised that the feeling of slipping away had gone. He had reached the end of that road and he had switched off. All he could see was a wall being built up around him, invisible to outsiders it would be, but impenetrable nonetheless. A natural process to deaden the pain when it came. If he truly loved Zoe then he couldn't expose her to an unopen shell, she wouldn't have the fun she wanted and he would lose her anyway. By dawn he had decided on his course of action. He would take her back home as planned and the following week explain that they would have to stop seeing each other. Zoe could have her freedom, there would be no pressure from him. For his part he could love her from afar, there could be no rancour in dreaming of what might have been. His slide had been into the basement of his emotions. To get out would require a lot of energy. He thought about a very long spiral stair case and the old saying was true; he would get over it.

The pale light of dawn grew into a grey morning. A few birds made a token effort at song outside. The coffee jar empty, he made a pot of tea. Zoe was still sleeping soundly. He thought how beautiful she looked, how she would fill the mornings of a man one day, a man *she* loved. He hoped she would be happy even though it could not be he. He had made her a cup of tea and was about to take it back to the kitchen. Before doing so he kissed her gently on the cheek. She awoke immediately.

Ray looked too much like he had been awake all night for him to deny it. Zoe was snug enough in a sleeping bag on the bed but the room itself was chilly. He shivered through a mixture of cold, fatigue and longing. She let him snuggle next to her sleeping bag and they lay there for what seemed like an age, motionless, silent. He shivered less and she twitched. Their lips met and in a frenzy their bodies locked together. Twice they made very physical love. Twice their bodies drew a supreme physical pleasure from each other. She convulsed with his gyrations until he finally shuddered in his orgasm.

Ray knew that it had been purely sexual, a meeting of bodies and not of minds. Even in the afterglow of satiety he was aware that the walls she had built to keep out his love were still there. But now there had been a quantum leap in the physical side of the relationship. The messages were no longer mixed, an actual physical desire had been displayed. He could no longer think of leaving her if he could await her heart on the soft cushion of sexual bliss. The walls he had built were walls of ignorance. He saw from the event only that which he wanted to see.

Ray saw Zoe only once again after they got back. In a period of remorse she told him she couldn't see him again. Bitter scenes followed. Friendships were cast onto the rocks. Ray remained in the basement for many months.

And there he was skivvying, working in a basement, his whole life, his career, in a basement and the walls he'd thrown up rapidly to protect himself from the intense pain of losing Zoe had kept him there.

Looking at the dated civil defence leaflets he mused how nations did exactly the same as individuals, threw up walls that impeded progression. He didn't get very far on that new tack but he had stopped thinking about Zoe for a brief spell, and that had never been easy over the months. He became aware that the heavy door to the street was open. The caretaker in the brown overalls was looking at him with a smile on his face.

"You've been miles away" he quipped.

Looking out into the sunshine of the street beyond the doors he mumbled a reply. The caretaker thought he said "Yes, I can see that now."

THE BROWN MACKINTOSH PART ONE

It may have been in *The Wagon and Horses* down Old Hill that Ray lost his first cloth cap but it could have been anywhere. That was a real pigeon fanciers number which he wore without fail at race meetings and on pub outings. His second cloth cap was a little less proletarian, it smacked of gentility and shooting small, seemingly harmless, furry animals. But you try telling a farmer that. The tailors from which he had bought it had an established pedigree of catering for such people's tastes. Nonetheless, he was pleased with his purchase, it was something of a piss-take. He stood in the doorway of the established tailors and patted the package in his pocket.

The sight of a young man running by up the High Street did nothing to capture Ray's attention until the lad veered sharply towards the indoor shopping arcade, bouncing off the rear wing of a Ford van in the process.

The collision seemed to stun him and he stopped in his tracks momentarily. Ray sucked in breath sharply through his teeth and tutted a "Careful!"

In the act of shaking his head Raymond Bragg looked the other way down the High Street. A steady stream of men, about ten in all, were running up the road and they all gave the impression that they were pushing themselves to the fullest extent of their capacities. It was an odd sight which refused to register at first.

Turning the other way again he saw the young man disappear into the shopping arcade, once more at speed. A balding man with a set, dour expression and a brown mac ran by at the head of the trailing pack. Close on his heels was a younger man wearing a black anorak and training shoes. They too disappeared into the arcade. One or two more followed then a fifth and sixth. Some of the stragglers seemed to have given up whatever it was they were after and returned, albeit a little breathless, to blending in with the grey thinning bands of shoppers.

An obese man wearing a donkey jacket and heavy boots ground to a halt in front of Ray. Breathing heavily, sweating profusely and purpling about the face he looked on the brink of a cardiac arrest. Between gulps for air he got out that the lad had just stolen something from a jewellers near the market place. A few more gulps then, "The police were waiting for him... a set up... a stake out." - Expressions stolen from American detective programmes - More gulps. The face returning to the rubicund normal of a beer drinker. "The police missed him. A balls up..." - An expression more native and natural from the man in difficulty.

There were two ways out of the shopping arcade. If the lad took the more obscure route to the gardens at the back then he would be on open ground and even if his pursuers were a long way back they would be able to see the direction in which he was heading. If he took the main route through then he would end up in Wolverhampton Street with a number of options and a possibility of escaping.

Without thinking why he was doing so, Raymond Bragg was running full pelt down into Wolverhampton Street. It was a much shorter route to the exit of the arcade via the streets. The obese man shouted good luck after him, no doubt relieved to be relieved of his duty.

About twenty yards before he got to the exit of the arcade the lad ran out. A man in a light grey anorak ran ten yards behind with a small shopping bag in his right hand. As Ray ran past the exit he heard someone shout "Stop him! The little bastard has just knocked an old woman over in here."

Ray thought that the man with the bag must have been chasing him because of that as he hadn't seen him in the original posse.

An Afro-Caribbean woman over the road looked on in disgust. "What all them white men chasing that black boy for?"

The lad put on a bit of a spurt. Ray felt himself going. Only the man with the bag was in the hunt now he thought.

They turned the corner right towards the Town Hall. Ray was only ten yards behind but with nothing left. The man with the bag was closer but he too must have felt he had lost the youth. Ray watched him give a last desperate swing of his bag as he stopped running. The bag caught the youth on the leg lightly and, as though he were obeying the rules of a playground game of tick, he too stopped.

For what seemed like an age the man with the bag and Raymond Bragg stood next to the youth who was impassive and didn't seem to even be out of breath. The balding man in the brown mac turned the corner and soon the handcuffs were on. No words were exchanged as the boy was led away.

Ray walked down the road a way with the man with the bag. "What exactly had he done?" Ray asked. The man muttered that he didn't know. Ray asked if he knew anything about the jewellers and the old woman in the arcade. The man obviously hadn't been aware of either event. He visibly cheered up at the news however. "Just saw everyone chasing the coon." he said "Can't let those bastards take over."

At once Ray wished he had been no part of it. He must have done something as he was placed under arrest Ray tried to reassure himself. He and the man with the bag went their separate ways.

THE BROWN MACKINTOSH PART TWO

Some things change rapidly others never seem to change at all. In the nine months since Raymond Bragg was last in town one thing had certainly changed, or else insanity was creeping in. He was looking for the record department on the top floor of Basils, the local version of Fenwicks of Bond Street. It had been there before he went away, right outside the coffee shop. How inconsiderate not to give a chap notice he thought as he paced around in the vain hope that light fittings and electrical goods would transmogrify into records. Five minutes had elapsed before he did the sensible thing and asked one of the assistants what had happened to the record department.

"Down in the basement now sir," the gracefully attired gentleman intimated with a faint suggestion that from his perspective, which approached middle age, the basement was where it belonged.

Ray took the elevator down to the basement which at first glance didn't appear to have altered. There was certainly no sign of any record department near the elevator. He infiltrated menswear, veered to the left and was confronted by lingerie. Always a touch coy about strolling past objects of such blatant sexual connotation he about faced and scanned the safer horizons of menswear.

A balding man in a brown mac looked up as Ray swept over gloves and scarves. They made eye contact and there was recognition. They knew each other from somewhere. But where? Ray thought for a moment. Why should he know that face? It wasn't too long before the yes that's it flashed across his mind. He was the policeman who had arrested the youth following that chase through town. Ray smiled and then looked back towards the man in the mac. Ray smiled again though not at the man for he knew he was watching him. Ah, he knows he has clocked me before but he can't remember where or when.

Walking out of menswear in the opposite direction to lingerie Ray spotted the record department in the far corner of the building. He made his way over to it purposefully.

Flicking through "Male Vocal D to F" Ray glanced up and there peering at "Country and Western Classics" with an unnatural nonchalance was the balding policeman in the brown mac. He looked up and immediately averted his eyes when he saw that Ray had turned his way.

Ray moved over to what he imagined, without looking, to be "Male Vocal G to K". He wasn't really looking at the albums now, just flicking through. He looked up again and the policeman had moved closer. This time he was on "T.V. Advertised Albums."

"Jesus H Christ!"Ray thought "He's tailing me!"

There was an outside chance that the man simply had a terrible taste in music but why would he have to watch Ray while pursuing it.

Ray picked up an album and took it to the counter. The policeman was making no pretence now, having moved away from the records he was watching Ray like a hawk.

Maybe not wishing to promenade through racks of négligées, knickers and bras had looked to a neutral observer suspicious. Suspicious enough for him to be deemed capable of a record department heist. Maybe... oh no! Ray thought, he can't think there's going to be a stick up.

The woman gave Ray his record and his change and thanked him for his custom. Ray walked out of the department, out of the store, out of the policeman's life for he stopped following him. Maybe he had suddenly remembered where he had seen Ray.

On his way home Ray was thinking about how many faces a copper must come across and how long they remember them for. It didn't matter. He took the record out of the bag and perused it with a certain amount of amazement. He didn't even like Stefan Grapelli!

Now there's one policeman he wouldn't forget in a hurry.

THE SINGING SHOPKEEPER

The plastic cup was now cold enough to hold - or at least no longer hot enough to cause severe burns. Robin Cruickshank loosened the small masses of pulped potato crisp which had adhered to his teeth with his tongue. He washed his mouth with the machine tea and grimaced at its tastelessness. He smoothed out the crisp packet and studied it before neatly folding it and placing it in the ashtray. He was deep in thought.

Being the same age I knew, almost with certainty what was coming next. There were two common topics of nostalgia amongst that section of the population whose childhood fell in the early 1960s. One was the contemporaneous childrens' television programmes, in particular the sci-fi "Supermarianation" programmes of Gerry and Silvia Anderson. "Stingray", "Thunderbirds" and the like. The second "do you remember" which occurred frequently was the little blue bag of salt found in packets of crisps.

Robin ran true to form. He looked up and said to me "Do you remember when..." I finished his sentence for him. Yes I could remember it well. Opening the packet hoping that the salt wrapped in a twist of blue paper wasn't right at the bottom, tipping the salt onto the crisps, clutching the bag shut again at the top and shaking vigorously before consuming the crisps which invariably became more and more salty the closer you got to the bottom of the packet.

I could have been no more than nine or ten when I was first made to recall those golden bygone days of the blue bag of salt. Ah, you used to get two in a packet sometimes. The thrill of finding yourself the possessor of two bags of salt, above your peers. The extra salt could make the top layer not quite so bland if shared out, or, if you were feeling contrary or not particularly generous on such an occasion you could tip both packets of salt on your own crisps to make them all as revoltingly salty as the bottom layer.

It was in an old sweet shop. I had gone into the establishment for a packet of crisps, ready salted. The old woman was very pleased I had chosen ready salted and not one of those new fangled flavours which in her view tasted nothing like cheese and nothing like onion. I was very pleased that I hadn't incurred her wrath. It was a shop that I hadn't been in before and it was one that I wouldn't go into again as the old woman had a hawkishly forbidding aspect. Her voice was stern as she lectured me on the efficacy of the potato crisp as it was in the days before *they* started flavouring them with chemicals.

The shop itself had little to recommend it visually. The corner shop was not yet the anachronism that the supermarket was to make it but this one was certainly an antique piece. The paintwork was a very dirty old brown, flaking to the point of non-existence in places, it had probably been applied between the the wars. Chipped enamel signs lay at the side advertising Spratts Dog Biscuits and Bovril. The former yellow and red letters on a royal blue background, the latter, red letters on a white background. All the colours were vivid but they were dirty and rusty where the enamel had chipped off. Weeds pushed through the pavement outside and moss filled the cracks left where cement had fallen away. The awning was decrepit and beyond repair. One enamel sign advertising Brookbond Tea still hung by rusty screws high up on the wall. The windows were dirty and the wares on display sunbleached. White letters had once advertised Cadbury's Bournville Drinking Chocolate on the glass but a lot of the letters were missing and those that remained were now a dirty cream in colour. It had been built as a shop and in its heyday would have been a general store for the women of the area. In the days before the refrigerator shopping would have been a daily event in a woman's life so excursions into town every day would have been a nonsense given a backcloth of labour intensive household chores. In short, the corner shop was a necessity. Things would have ground to a hungry halt had they not existed.

The decaying little outpost of those different days remained even though it had outlived its usefulness. Homes were full of labour saving devices, women had longer leisure hours, refrigerators meant that food could be stored for much longer periods, the cars outside the houses ensured mobility. Travelling to town once a week for the whole weeks shopping was no longer a nonsense, it made for even more leisure time. The corner shop was outdated in the general scheme of things.

The little old lady proprietor no longer stocked anything like vegetables, or perishables of any sort. The sole function of the shop was now sweets and ice cream... and crisps. Anything which the local kids would drop in and spend their pennies on. In kids and sweets the old lady had a never ending market. Although the shop itself was foreboding and her manner forbidding it had been there for many years and must have done some business to remain open. "Crisps. Yes my boy. Not like they used to be. Smiths, Smiths crisps. They were the best. And no chemicals!"

I left with my packet of crisps which weren't Smiths at all but at that time I imagined that shops were supplied by magic so I didn't question her advocating something she didn't sell. I wasn't at the age where I questioned things. The old crisps were the thing she had put across at great length. I remember agreeing with her. I also remember making a point to take my pennies elsewhere.

The next time I took any notice of that particular corner shop was a few years later when I was taken completely aback by the fact that it had been painted. It looked like a new building. It was the bright colours which did the trick, a light blue and white gloss. There were sacks full of vegetables outside and a set of scales on a bench. The awning had been patched up and was used as a shelter or shade for the vegetables.

A new husband and wife team were in charge. A sign said simply "O'Rourkes".

Henry O'Rourke and his wife Dolly were the ones responsible for breathing new life into the decaying old shop. The name was somewhat deceptive in that any Irish connection between Henry O'Rourke and his forbears had been lost in the mists of time. His family was Black Country and he was Dudley born and bred. He had been a runner when he was young, in the days before the war, and had won medals as a distance man. After serving in Europe in the war he worked at an engineering company which relied on Austins for the bulk of its work. In the early 1970s there were such things as redundancies though they weren't the commonplace they would become. Henry O'Rourke was made redundant and bought Astley's old corner shop with his redundancy money. I hadn't been in since the tutorial on the potato crisp. I don't know whether it was the fresh look of the place or the apparently cheery disposition of Henry and Dolly whose whistles and songs could be heard from the street which beckoned me to cross once more the portals of the shop.

Henry was singing when I entered. "Just Molly and me and the baby makes three...." It was very much tidier inside, a grocery store now, not just a sweet shop. It was very much lighter too. Vague images of black-out curtains and gas mantles receded from my mind along with my other associations with the establishment. I felt at once perfectly safe to purchase a packet of crisps without fear of a lecture on the subject.

Henry and Dolly had a way with people and they even stretched their effort of trying to establish a regular clientele to the neighbourhood kids. I don't know whether Henry knew or maybe it was just an educated guess but he dropped in on his first sale to this kid he'd never seen before "Now the Baggies."

For my part I was fascinated by this middle aged couple of average height and build, whose clothes and hair were what one would expect of their generation but sang and whistled and shared their neighbourliness with the local children. Learning that he too was a lover of West Bromwich Albion started a long friendship.

Henry covered most of the shops opening hours but Dolly did a fair stint over the week. It was very much a team effort. I came to spend many hours there talking football, the Albion greats of the past - Old Joe Smith lived down the road I was reliably informed before I was told of the great full back pair of Joe Smith and Jesse Pennington. Henry was two clear eras older than my father in terms of the club's history, but his sporting interests didn't end there. Apparently I was the right height and agile enough but I needed a bit of meat on my frame before I could become a boxer. Henry and Dolly always had time for me no matter how full the shop was and sometimes it bulged at the seams, such was the trade they built up on good will. It was in such a busy period that I became part of the team, helping lighten the load by weighing out vegetables and tipping them into the customers bags before they went back inside and paid. In that period of apprenticeship I suppose that Henry came to the conclusion that I could be trusted. My duties stretched to the other side of the counter as I was first invited for cups of tea in the back room and then allowed to serve people. It was a great bond of trust, my taking money from customers and giving change back. I was to Henry and Dolly in real terms only another kid from the street. But the friendship grew for as well as an interest in sport we had something else in common. I was at an age where I had started to question things. I was starting to develop a political awareness. From a working class and Labour family I had a socialist perspective. Over many cups of tea in the back room of the corner shop that perspective was focused by Henry O'Rourke.

The Tories were in power at the time. Edward Heath had moved into 10 Downing Street and many thought that it was the housewives exercising their right for the first time that put him there. On the eve of the election he had promised to cut prices at a stroke and the housewives were felt to have bought that promise. Henry saw a lot of housewives. Most of his customers were housewives from the neighbourhood. Some would come from the well to do area across the main road a distance but most were what might be described as working class women. Some were unrepentent, others were silent and a third group admitted to feeling duped at voting for the Tories when after a year or so the stroke at which the prices were to fall had yet to materialise. There were of course ronk-Labour women and the ones from the well to do area who came to the corner shop because they liked the personal touch were positively Land of Hope and Glory. Like a good businessman Henry never talked politics in the shop with his customers. People of all political shades were greeted with My Blue Heaven or Nelly Dean come what may. He used to listen however, the prejudices of the wealthy, the petty snobbery of the aspirant bourgeois. They can't fool me he would tell me in confidence. Though a lot of women now did their shopping at the supermarket in town many of them couldn't break the habit of a lifetime and stop their daily outing to the shop. Much of Henry's custom was women out for a chin wag who would buy only a few items, the deliberate oo-I-forgot from the weekly shopping list.

Henry knew that he had come in late to a dying institution. The supermarkets represented big business and he saw it as a bad business. "There's no room left for the small guy now. They're pushing us right out of it and they won't stop until they've succeeded."

Sometimes he would come right out and advocate an economy approaching communism as the way out of the mess. That was how sinister he saw the mass marketing of big business. I don't know whether Dolly shared his apprehension about the way things were going for small business but neither of them showed it up front. The shop itself was a joyous place. They achieved a regular custom on a site which had been run down virtually to extinction. As well as the women there were the men who always called in for their cigarettes. Despite the regular trade, they operated on the knife edge of low profits.

Part of the O'Rourke trade was the Asian immigrants. Like a good many white working class, he was distrustful of them. Like many solid Labour voters he would enthuse about Enoch Powell. The paradox of an egalitarian party's bulk support being racist had yet to cause problems. "They know the language when they need to use it and its no speakee Ingleesh when it suits." On other occasions he would have long conversations with another member of the same community and say afterwards "Oh. he's alright, they are not all bad." He sang for them too so on the surface he treated them equally.

I used to go down on Saturday afternoons when Albion were away to keep him company. Dolly was helping less and less. She had become tired of late. We'd talk about sport and politics or just plain gossip. He never convinced me that the '51 side were better than the '68 one or of the soundness of Enoch Powell's policies.

One Friday night I was walking down the hill with a girl. It was quite late. Henry had always reckoned that I was a dark horse as he'd seen them in the shop looking at me. "I can tell you know." The sign had gone. The shop was boarded up. I had only been there the previous Saturday and he hadn't said a word. There had been no good-bye. But thinking about it there had been no hello either just an acceptance into the world of the singing shopkeeper. That world like the corner shop had passed for good.

I heard of him about a year later. He had been doing some gardening and some caretaking. Dolly had had a stroke but was recovering. He still whistled and sang but the edge had gone from his voice. No room in this world for the small guys any more. It seemed like being the singing shopkeeper had become too much for him.

There's a Post Office on the site now. I go down there to buy stamps, but nobody sings.

A HAPPY ATHEIST

The curtains were almost fully drawn. She had pulled them to so that the bright sunlight wouldn't make the watching of the lunchtime news next to impossible. She was Hoovering now. It seemed a little darker outside she thought as she looked up for a moment.

Just then the sun came back from behind the clouds and an intense shaft of light broke through the gap in the curtains. It hurt her eyes and she averted them towards the floor while the spots disappeared. There was a time when she would have cursed but that was before it happened, she was much more thoughtful now - about everything. It had been like that when she first recognised the Almighty. He had been there all along and when she first saw Him it had been in a blinding flash, seen the light as it were. And He had been good enough to remind her by sending the sun through the clouds at that time when she was beginning to forget about the task at hand that very afternoon.

The world was full of sceptics so the vacant looks, indifference or downright rudeness which the door to door canvassing by Rose and her fellow Jehovah's Witnesses elicited was accepted as par for the course. But out of the multitude of sceptics there would be one or two who were ready, willing or indeed waiting to be saved. After the final battle His witnesses would remain to dwell in His Kingdom. It was their solemn duty to root out those destined for the path. To leave blind those with the potential to see would be an unforgivable sin. The rudeness of those who would be permanently blind was nought against the few who could be saved. That afternoon they were to visit one of the few who had potential. It was so exciting. As well as being so important.

He was a young man in his early thirties and he lived alone. He wore a slightly dishevelled look no matter what time of day they visited and as their visits were frequent they had fully tested their observations. His listening to them gave them the feeling of hope for him, someone actually listening to what they had to say was always a good sign for all they had to say either overtly or covertly was their message. He was obviously well educated and well travelled and the arguments he gave would, on the surface, tend to give the impression that he did not agree with them. He claimed he was an atheist but Rose couldn't believe that, he came over as being far too sympathetic in nature to honestly hold such a heathen philosophy. Then there was the other question. A sense of loneliness, a sense of loss surrounded him. That was the real reason behind Rose putting him on her list of strong possibilities and visiting once a month for a long chat. He filled her with a sadness. She liked him. His arguments stimulated her, tested her faith. Her faith had proved unshakeable but, alas, so had his. She was going to make her previous visit the last as she was filled with remorse that he would not see the light. He seemed to have his own faith but he was an atheist and atheism wasn't a faith, atheism was negative, not believing, refuting the evidence and saying God wasn't there. That was reason enough to be sad for him but a further sadness that he had a name and she didn't know what it was. He whom she felt certain to be, behind the facade, a very sad person, had no faith and he had no name. The thought of elevating things to a personal level had a disquieting effect on Rose and there hung her new sadness. Had she become interested in him the person and had she thereby forsaken her responsibility to him?

But on what was to have been the last visit it had happened. They had managed to sell him a book and he had promised to read it. It was the Jehovah's Witness answer to the argument of evolution. He used to make her so cross. "I'll not make evolution my bible" he'd say. "Evolution's a theory not an established fact." Surely there had to be hope for someone who wouldn't use science as a straight alternative to religion. But he'd go and spoil it all by following on coolly to their eager promptings that therefore there must be a God with "God is only a theory too, not an established fact."

On that last visit he conceded that he had not read much evidence from the anti-evolution lobby which was growing in the States. He said that he had recently read a review of a book called "The Blind Watchmaker" which challenged the concept of an intelligent designer but little else on the subject of late. Neither Rose nor her companion had heard of it. Rose offered to lend him their book but he said that he would buy it as it was only a few pounds. With that purchase Rose's dark thoughts about her own motives were dispelled or at least displaced as she could pin her hopes for him on the book. Maybe in reading it he would see his error. He read a lot therefore it was not difficult to suppose that God would make Himself known to him through the pages of a book. Rose hoped that that had been the case as her companion rang the door bell.

He seemed a little tired, a little more drawn than usual and certainly sadder. It was no good for a man to be on his own Rose thought immediately, hoping that she meant that no man was alone if he had God but she wasn't sure that her feelings weren't altogether more secular. He looked preoccupied, it took him a while before recognition set in. He raised a cosmetic smile.

"We can go away if you're not feeling well" Rose said which drew a frown from her companion.

He shook his head as if clearing it of a fog. "No" he said hesitantly. "Look I'm sorry. I was miles away."

There was a ten second silence which seemed interminable. Rose's companion that day was Jill. She was new and keen and far from impressed with this bedraggled seemingly bewildered specimen who had been described as a great hopeful. She was about to launch into a lecture which would have had far more to do with class prejudice than the wisdom of belonging to her church when Rose and the man spoke simultaneously.

"I've been coming here so often and I don't even know your name. What is it?"

"You've been coming here so often and still I keep you outside my home. Why don't you come in?"

The result was unintelligible. They both laughed, more of a giggle than a guffaw. Rose composed herself uneasily as Jill had opened her Jehovah's Witness Bible which was already full of underlinings in pencil which were used not only in answer to the questions and jibes of sceptics but also for her own edification and further enlightenment.

Rose asked again "Your name?" John told her his name but felt no better about things on learning that it was from the bible, a fact that hadn't hitherto escaped his attention. He invited them into the warm as it had turned quite chilly with a sharp wind blowing and the cloud cover complete. Jill's frown was beginning to look etched, such had its depth become. She might have been a new convert, but this was most irregular to her mind. Rose seemed to be flirting and was about to enter the house. The bible was open and Jill twitching. It was something about temptation. Rose checked herself and opened her attempt to bring John into the fold with a hopeful question about the book before Jill could deliver the rhetoric.

John said that he had read the book and had found it interesting though in parts terribly biased, in parts misleading (especially the mathematical arguments) and in some places downright mendacious. Rose had to admit that she didn't know what mendacious was but wasn't upset on learning that John thought that the book lied a little bit. It was all too soft a sell for Jill. She started questioning John about evolution. She knew all the patter - and the requisite references in the bible. The evidence is incomplete, all the counter evidence. Genesis clearly states. Seven days isn't meant to be taken literally. John was unmoved. Jill asked him what he thought. He paused and then he told her patiently. She had him. The moment he started she knew she had him.

"How do you know all this is true?"

"I don't, it's only a theory. A theory with a lot of supportive evidence."

"The answers are here in the bible. This isn't theory, its fact."

"How do you know?"

"Because it's the word of God"

"Who is just a theory" John interjected before disappearing.

He returned moments later with a copy of "The Origin of Species".

"Here you are look" he said leafing through. ""You are not the only ones who can look at books." He wasn't as adroit as a Jehovah's Witness at finding the passages which suited his purpose but eventually he found it. "Here it is. Charles Darwin himself. The evidence is far from complete. He knew only too well it was a theory. Theories require verification. Evolution has yet to be verified."

"So you don't believe in evolution then?"

Rose was confused. "You don't believe in God because you do believe in evolution and now you say you don't."

"Its not a question of replacing religion totally with science as, I'm afraid, a lot of scientists have done."

Jill was not confused, she was livid. They were wasting their time, the man was an atheist, he believed in nothing, no God, no sense to the world. She was about to vent her spleen when John again got in first.

"You are wrong. It's not a case of me not believing in God. I do believe you see. I do have a belief just he same as you have a belief. It's just that my belief is the exact opposite of yours. I do believe that there is no God."

There was a stoney silence. John pressed on.

"Another difference, it seems to me, is that I respect your beliefs so why can't you respect mine."

"But we do" they chimed in unison, though for different reasons.

"Then what are you doing here trying to make your beliefs my beliefs."

Rose was quite relieved that John did in fact believe in something. Jill was most unsympathetic with those beliefs.

"You can't believe in nothing. What if something happens, a tragedy say, how would belief in nothing help you? Faith helps people through such crises. What do you think your philosophy could do for you in that situation? Have you ever thought of that?"

Jill was beginning to sound doctrinaire to Rose, not at all like the caring face of religion that Rose hoped she portrayed herself. It reminded Rose of the Trotskis, as she called them, she used to know from her life before revelation came to her. All self-opinionation and absolutely no feeling for the individual. She sensed that John was becoming impatient with the situation. She hoped that she had never come over as being so pushy, so apparently intolerant, so rude. Jill had become personal in questioning his outlook on life. Rose wanted to stop it but couldn't find the words.

John listened to Jill with an ever decreasing level of patience, he kept on glancing at Rose hoping that she might intervene but she looked decidedly uncomfortable in the presence of this zealot. John had hoped to persuade Rose that knocking on people's doors trying to ram religion down their throats was no way to carry on for someone who displayed a reasonable degree of openness of mind. They had, over the months, had some lively discussions, he had enjoyed them, he hoped that Rose had. Jill was doing the persuading now. For the first time in her years of standing on doorsteps Rose felt embarrassed. Embarrassed to be there doing the work of God. Were Jill's actions the work of God?

John eventually snapped but not into a temper. The words which came were not a verbal assault, but a measured story. John had told no strangers because it was none of their business. He eventually decided to tell his story because he no longer felt Rose to be a stranger. Jill was attacking him for looking sad. He couldn't possibly claim to be happy with life because he looked so sad.

At that John looked at Rose and said, "It's funny that you should come today. Today I'm sad because anniversaries are bad."

It had been two years to the day since his wife and two children had been wiped out in a car crash. They had only been going to the local shops for some ice cream. A stolen car full of joy riders on the wrong side of the road. Mother and son died instantly but the young daughter held on to life for a week. There was the guilt. He had forgotten to get the ice cream earlier. The pain of the loss. The grieving process and, because of the tragic circumstances the ever present anger and frustration at the unanswerable Why Me!

Jill kept on trying to butt in. Reality for her, and therefore everyone else, was what *she* knew. The experiences of others didn't enter into the equation. If they didn't agree with Jill then it was their interpretation of their experiences that were flawed. John took no notice. What a person experienced and what a person felt were realities, contradiction of them was ridiculous. He was telling it all for Rose's benefit.

Rose was never a person to deny another their life experiences. It was a revelation - though not a heart fluttering one, as God had been - that the man's outlook on life had helped him through. There had been great sadness in his life but he had lived on to lead a relatively happy and fruitful existence. He was a happy atheist.

The interview ended with Rose shuffling away in a very tearful mood. John bought a copy of Watchtower as it seemed the only way of ridding himself of Jill who, he was sure, would have stayed on the doorstep lecturing even if he had shut the front door in her face. He had half a mind to ask Rose to come back another day but to leave Jill at the tabernacle or whatever it was they met in. He thought better of being so overtly rude. But a zealot can't help but be rude.... so perhaps there would be no harm done....

Rose did a lot of thinking over the next week. A post-Armageddon Utopia full of people like Jill didn't seem such a good idea as it had done. Maybe if people could learn to get along with each other then the world would be a better place. Someone like Jill, why God had chosen her heaven only knew. She could well precipitate Armageddon before God was ready. But getting on with people, learning to accept differences. That had to start in the home....

Neither Rose nor John attended any church. They were eventually married in a register office. She was a devout believer in God's wisdom. John, well, he was a happier atheist than he had been before Rose came into his life.

BALDWIN'S MONUMENT

Stanley Baldwin had no interest in politics but couldn't really escape being connected with it as he shared the name of the incumbent Prime Minister. Our Stanley's interests were drinking, gambling, whippets and pigeons, though not necessarily in that order of priority. He was married but women fell somewhere between work and football in the scheme of things and as he professed allegiance to Aston Villa, football ranked about two pegs of a crib board higher than politics which had pegged just one hole and had only achieved that recently thanks to that knave of a Prime Minister having the same name. In short, his bosses and his wife saw much less of him than did the publicans and bookmakers and characters of similar persuasion.

Politics wasn't to escape his attention forever. One night he had a skinful of ale in a licensed establishment in which the gaffer suffered from an inability to tell the time. This was no chance thing as Stanley was quite particular in choosing to purchase his drink only in those establishments where a similar disability was displayed by the landlord. Stanley was accustomed to late drinking but on this particular occasion he had more than usual and forgot to visit the urinal at the back of the pub before meandering home.

Stanley wasn't staggering along his way but he was perhaps a little less mindful than normal, especially when he was taken short and a piss became an urgent requirement. Stanley was happy however. No sooner had nature called than Stanley replied. He unbuttoned his flies and pointed himself at the wall.

The relief was immense but as he was buttoning up his flies, he felt a hand on his shoulder. Two special constables had witnessed him voiding urine in a public place. Now Stanley might have been a bit of a lad, a touch belligerent and a touch inconsiderate maybe but it was undisputed in the circles in which he mixed that he was as honest as the day was long and never broke the law. The ignominy of a night in the cells and being hauled up before the magistrate the next day was almost too much for his long suffering wife. He had been late on so many occasions that she had long come to expect him when she saw him, but to have a policeman come to the front door! At first she feared the worst.

Stanley soon sobered up in the cells. He was working on his defence which, as he himself couldn't possibly be guilty of any misdemeanour, must centre around negligence on the part of someone else. He couldn't blame the two special constables for picking on him, they were just doing their job and he did have the temerity to take a leak before their very eyes.

The distance between his own house and the public house he had been using was great. Far too great for someone taken short after a long libation. There wasn't a public urinal where he committed his act no, granted. But there ought to be one. The borough council were very much at fault in this. That was Stanley Baldwin's defence.

Stanley Baldwin's natural habitat was the bar. He was a bit of a talker, very much the raconteur in fact which led his cronies to speak in jest that he should become a politician. Such suggestions always angered Stanley and often elicited an acerbic response from his murderous wit. As the frequency of the suggestion increased with the arrival of his namesake at Number Ten, the venom of his reply led many to believe that he was something of a radical.

Stanley had heard, somewhere in his past, courtrooms referred to as the bar. It was not surprising then that he felt most at home before the magistrates even though in comparison theirs was more of an off-licence than the fully fledged hostelry of the Old Bailey. With taproom wit he expounded his defence to the magistrates as his tearful wife clutched a handkerchief in the public gallery. Their worships listened in taciturn bewilderment at the entertainment before them. They took into account that Stanley had never been before them in the past but clearly hoped that he would call again soon. They fined him £2. The clerk of the court recorded that he was also bound over to keep the peace for 12 months but this was really the chairman of the bench having a little fun in telling Stanley to keep his piss to himself. The bench tittered but the clerk was humourless. He suggested that if Stanley found the council deficient in its provision of amenities for the community then he had every right to stand for election and change things. Stanley left the court room in a red faced rage. He had just entered politics.

At first no one believed him, least of all the local pigeon fanciers, publicans and whippet racers. His wife was the first to take him seriously as he spent more time at home studying books borrowed from the library. For the first week Mrs Baldwin held an internal debate as to which was the greater shock; Stanley being at home more or Stanley borrowing books from the library. The visit from the ward councillor told her that he was not in jest saying that he would stand in the next local elections as an independent candidate. The local councillor freely gave advice on how to stand as he thought it was all part of some big joke. Stanley obtained the necessary number of nominations and did all that was required to become a candidate. The major parties thought well, Stanley is making his point right enough, but he isn't a serious challenger. Some chap with a bee in his bonnet about being caught voiding urine in a public place isn't going to cut much ice with the public.

Now this was something of an error of judgement for Stanley ran his campaign along the lines of there being a chronic lack of amenities within the ward and a chronic lack of things being done about it. In a ward with few amenities the verity of Stanley Baldwin's argument could hardly go unnoticed. His campaign had the support of every publican in the ward not to mention all those late night boozers who had voided urine in a public place and with the grace of God gone undetected. There was also a general feeling that it would be nice to have a councillor with the same name as the Prime Minister. It was the major parties who came unstuck. Stanley Baldwin was duly elected councillor at the local elections and his campaign in the council chamber began on day one for more amenities within the ward and within the borough. He headed his list with a public urinal which would be situated on the exact spot of his arrest.

Now Stanley Baldwin didn't just edge into the council chamber by a few odd votes, it was a huge turnout and his victory was a landslide. Secret meetings were held at the behest of the local leaders of all the major parties. Something had to be done and done quickly otherwise the council chamber would soon be full of jumped up bar-flies who had a grudge against authority. The situation transcended party rivalries.

The council unanimously voted for a public urinal to be built on the site of Stanley Baldwin's arrest. The work commenced immediately. Councillor Baldwin officially opened the building and took the first leak in the new facility. It was his last official act as a councillor for he attended no more meetings, saw no more constituents and took no further interest in politics save the occasional reminder that he shared the name of the incumbent Prime Minister.

The urinal became known as Baldwin's Monument. Few councillors get their own monument after so short a tenure of office. Then again few councillors share the name of the incumbent Prime Minister.

* Baldwin is fictitious but there was a "Bodin's Monument" I'm told!

TIM THE TATTER

Can...I...do...it...Can...I...do...it
I-think-I-can-I-think-I-can
I'vedoneitI'vedoneitI'vedoneit

Twenty-eight times daily the Dodger's engine spoke the ditty to any who cared to listen as it laboured up the steep incline from the low level at Dudley Port to the station in town. The Dudley Port Dodger kept the town in touch with the main line.

From the station to the High Street was another long hill which was steep enough if you happened to be going up it. As it was overshadowed by the castle it was called Castle Hill. Cyclists going down were warned of its danger while trams and motorised vehicles trundled up it without the poetic accompaniment the Dodger enjoyed. Horses who had to make the last leg of the journey to Dudley must have cursed, especially if they had a full load on.

Tim the Tatter was known throughout the town - as was his horse Bess. Tim had had a good round at the old munition worker's huts and his cart was precariously loaded with heavy junk.

Now Bess had been up Castle Hill many times before and was quite used to it taking a long time, not to mention a lot of huff and puff. She was also used to not receiving the least bit of help from Tim who would sit on the cart all the way up the hill, a battered trilby hat perched on his balding pate as he watched the world go slowly by. Bess also knew that while Tim could be cruel to humans he was never cruel to horses in general and her in particular even though it often appeared that he was.

The load that day was heavy and the portly Tim made it heavier still. Bess had a sweat on and snorted loudly as she came to all but a standstill. A bunch of balloons tied on at the front fluttered in the breeze.

A passing constable shook his head in disbelief. 'He'll be the death of that horse, the scoundrel,' he thought. He produced his notebook and pencil.

"Now then Tim! You've got too much of a load on for that poor horse," he barked sternly. "Lighten it or I'll book you."

With the alacrity of a conjurer Tim produced a pin and burst one of the balloons.

"Is that better constable?" Tim replied as Bess got her second wind and started off again. Tim knew that the hill and the load were well within the capabilities of the horse. So did Bess, but it didn't stop her wishing from time to time that her master would get off his arse - as she had often heard him bid others - and walk!

* There are many Tim the Tatter stories in circulation in the Black Country. The Black Country Bugle recorded a number (including this one which my father would frequently tell) in the autumn of 1991.

GRANDMA'S APPARITION

Due to Grandma's proclivity for frequent omission of the indefinite article from the spoken word, confusion sometimes reigned on the few occasions that it slipped into her speech. On one particular occasion it hadn't though I assumed it had and was, as a result, for a long time bewildered by teachers of English taking exception to my stating the to-ings and fro-ings of "paritions" in my ghost stories.

Have you ever seen a ghost Grandma? - Yes son. When I was young I saw apparition.

An easy enough mistake for a child to make...... Grandma was a young woman when it happened. It was in the days of rows of two up and two down terraces with common courtyards at the rear accommodating the brew-house, the wash-house and the other house wherein natural functions were performed. Grandma wasn't even ma, let alone grand, she was Tilly who had to get up early every morning to walk the 3 miles to work at the brickyards.

One dark morning before setting off to work Tilly was in the third house of the courtyard performing one of nature's functions. Someone else was up early for from the brew-house adjacent, the smell of bread baking wafted through to Tilly's nostrils making her feel hungry. A few minutes later, on her way past, Tilly looked through the open door to see Mrs Rogers from four doors away facing the other way and singing softly to herself.

"Morning Mrs Rogers," Tilly shouted without stopping. From the corner of her eye she thought she saw Mrs Rogers turn but didn't hear any reply.

After a day of hard graft, loading and unloading the brick kilns, stacking the bricks and anything else the foreman directed, Tilly made her way home, ravenously hungry as usual. Tea was a scanty affair as there appeared to be no bread. Tilly had the solution however.

"Mrs Rogers will have some bread, she was baking early this morning. It smelt lovely, I nearly asked for some then."

Tilly's mother and father had gone quiet. Granny nodded knowingly in the corner while sucking on her clay pipe. Father broke the silence.

"I don't think it was Mrs Rogers you saw our Tilly."

Tilly didn't question her father as he had made the statement in such a way as to say that it wasn't to be questioned. The explanation was quick in coming.

"Mrs Rogers passed away in the night."

There was another period of uneasy silence as Tilly fidgeted in the knowledge that she saw what she saw while her father gazed on in the knowledge that he knew what he knew and there was to be no nonsense.

Granny took her pipe from her mouth to deliver her verdict on the matter.

"Most likely our Tilly see'd apparition."

So it was that Grandma would say that when she was young she saw apparition and that was an end to it.

TOMMY STONE'S SEND OFF

The "Lime Green Flyer" they had called it. It was certainly distinctive if nothing else and a distinctive car was quite a possession for a teenager, especially so considering a Morris 1100 was a singularly undistinctive model. Originally it had been Grandad's car and when pristine it had been the dark "Connaught Green" which looked decidedly better on tanks and other army vehicles than private cars. Sister had possession for a time until she got married and while it was in her keep a friend of her fiancé, who was deemed by some as holding not quite the full ticket, sprayed the clonal quasi-army green Morris with a vivid lime green paint to produce a means of transport singular in the town, the Lime Green Flyer. Naturally I was sad to lose it when its days were numbered. Perhaps a little less flying over hump-backed bridges and the engine mountings would have lasted longer. It was the rear sub frame that was going to cost the money though so the family elders decided that the car would best be scrapped. Reluctantly I agreed that the Lime Green Flyer had to go and proceeded to do nothing about it. I was told a few days before the M.O.T. was about to expire to go to the public bar of *The Tree* and see Tommy Stone about it.

Tommy Stone was the rough diamond, wit, raconteur, and underworld interface of the Kates Hill circuit of bars. Some said that his fraternity were jailbirds and layabouts but they all seemed to treat everyone decently in the locale and with genuine respect. Tommy himself had never been "inside" and was far from a layabout though no one can ever remember him having an official job. Tommy claimed from the social yes, he was entitled to it he would have pointed out, but any work he did do was under the condition that the tax man didn't get a percentage. Tommy Stone lived on good fortune and he'd do anything; clean windows, paint houses, move furniture and, apparently, scrap cars, as the situation arose. Such jobs never lasted very long so there was little point in signing off and signing back on again - Tommy liked his book-keeping was kept simple, there was no book! Tommy seemed to remain solvent however as he was constantly to be found during licensing hours in some bar or another or else at his accountants which were of the turf variety.

He granted me an audience at the modest expense to my exchequer of half a pint of mild. Something of a consultant really in the matter of moving objects around, I suppose, he had a right to a small fee for his services and being in a pub at night was for him during office hours. Tommy could take the Lime Green Flyer off my hands. He nodded and contorted his face so as to make himself appear shrewd. It was the closest I had been to him. I knew him to look at and knew of him by reputation and here I was doing a deal with him, this tall man with a permanently ruddy complexion, sharp features and short black Brylcreamed hair. He said he'd give me a tenner for the car after what seemed like an age of silent deliberation. It seemed like a good deal but I remained silent as I was expecting a catch.

"It helps yoe out and it meks a few bob for me. Everybody happy." Tommy put in philosophically.

I accepted the offer and Tommy pulled a Ten Pounds note from his wallet at a time when Ten Pounds notes weren't a common sight particularly. I was waiting for the tenner to disappear in some sleight-of-hand but it didn't. I mumbled something about the log book but Tommy pursed his lips and shook his head vigorously but that was his little joke.

"Leave it in the motor," he said.

Next day the Lime Green Flyer was gone.

Now while some might have thought that Tommy spent an inordinate length of time playing cards or dominoes for money or gambling on anything that moved, they would have been overlooking the tremendous amount of work he did for charity. Granted, Tommy Stone was the charity for which he most frequently did his good works but good works he did do. In many a pub there wasn't a collection tin that he didn't organise and while some people got indignant that Tommy and his fraternity were in all probability taking a percentage, it had to be weighed against the fact that Tommy and his fraternity got more money put into the boxes and thus got the charities concerned far more in the way of donations from the good people of Kates Hill than had those boxes stood gathering dust on the bar. Most of the collections were with bona fide sealed tins but those for the darts or crib team card which were collected in a pint mug or on a tray were the cause of most concern. Any complaints about the frequency of such collections and the infrequency of any announced winner generally ended with the plaintiff receiving the evening's star prize, a change in luck doing wonders for both morale and morals. One time Tommy took a tray round the bar in *The Tree* and came right out with it, "I'm skint. It's for my beer." No one could argue with that for integrity. On another occasion he stood outside *The Tree* on a summer evening and struggled with a huge map, asking strangers where he was.

Tommy was known to be full of tricks. *The Tree* crib team had been playing at a pub called *The West End* on the other side of town. Tommy and his fraternity, who were both the crib and darts teams for *The Tree*, wandered into *The Fighting Man* beside the park wherein I was entertaining a young lady. They treated us to drinks all night as well as an endless stream of badinage punctuated by various items purloined from *The West End* falling from their pockets. The following weekend I stood at the bar in *The Tree* admiring a new, or rather, old ornate rosewood clock which had been acquired from somewhere. An old stager next to me commented that there used to be a clock just like it in *The West End*, so Tommy's charitable nature extended to keeping his local furnished in a suitable manner.

Tommy was seen as mischievous rather than malevolent. He was a rough diamond to his own generation and a character to learn from for the young. My last dealing with Tommy Stone was of a public holiday Tuesday. I went into the bar of *The Tree* on the lunchtime and it was full of Tommy's fraternity who seemed cheery enough. One of the women held a tray in front of me before I had had chance to even order a pint. I asked what it was in aid of and was given the reply "Tommy Stone's funeral. He died in the night."

Well, it was bank holiday and everyone would be in a jolly mood and while I hadn't heard of using Tommy's demise before as a means of extracting beer money from the populace I was quite sure it wasn't its first time in operation. Now while I gave the effort full marks for ingenuity, I was a bit low on ready cash myself so I told the woman that she was mistaken in thinking that I would stand for the three card trick. She wasn't offended by my error as a friend of my father verified that Tommy Stone had indeed passed on in the night. I put some money on the tray. In his passing Tommy Stone had become a legend.

Doubtless there was a funeral at which his fraternity celebrated his life as was their wont. But was it any way for a Black Country legend to depart. Had some of Tommy's young admirers had their way he would have lain in state for three days in Yate's Wine Lodge in Dudley market place. Then, at the appointed hour the coffin would have been placed on a dray waggon and draped with the flag recently stolen from Hanson's brewery. He would then have been taken at walking speed along Dixons Green past *The Tree* wherein, upon the cortége passing, as at every pub en route, the dominoes and beer glasses would cease to rattle for one minute. Also, on passing *The Tree*, there would have been a fly past by the pigeons from all the local lofts. From *The Tree* the cortége would make its way down to Bumble Hole canal basin where the coffin would be loaded onto an old barge to be cast adrift then set alight by flaming darts thrown by *The Tree* team.

That would be a send off fit for a Black Country folk hero. Sadly however, send offs like that don't exist in reality and as the year 2000 approaches, characters like Tommy Stone will soon cease to be a reality too.

---

* *Based on a well known character of Kates Hill. As with all characters he became something of a legend and sorting out the fact from the fiction is difficult when the only facts available are the commonly held fictions.*

STEEL TOWN MYTH

The Stobbarts had been steelworkers for three generations. Great grandfather had worked at small blast furnaces in the region. Grandfather had started in the smaller enterprises but finished his working life at the massive Round Oak Works in Brierley Hill. Father's working life was spent entirely at Round Oak but that life ended prematurely with the mass closures of steel works throughout Britain. Round Oak being shed came as a surprise as it followed by only a few years a huge government investment of millions of pounds to make it one of the most up to date plants in Europe. The jewel in the crown of British Steel some called it. John Stobbart could only watch on the sidelines as the community went into decline. The only source of comfort in his autumn years was that his son had had a decent education. He was a little dismayed when Paul decided to follow his forbears into the steel industry.

"Steel in this country is finished" John warned him ruefully.

With his degree, Paul was to be management. He was shown round the plant he was to work at by an old manager who had worked his way up from the shop floor, a very rare breed indeed in a decimated industry. In the intense heat of the works Paul was shown things he had been made aware of many years before by his father. The old manager littered the tour with anecdotes, the steel town myths, which he had fallen out of his cradle listening to.

"What with the Health and Safety at Work legislation things are a lot safer. You don't get the accidents you used to."

They were clad in safety helmets, goggles, protective clothing and heavy shoes. His father wouldn't have been dressed up like a spaceman when he first started, Paul thought.

"See that gantry up there over the vat?"

Paul looked up towards the roof and saw the walkway which ran near the edge of a vat which more often than not contained molten steel. He knew what was coming next.

"When I first started here, which is more years than I care to remember, there was only a railing on one side and not a very high one. One day someone was running along there and he must have slipped. Tumbled into the molten steel. His mate ran along with a great big pole and what do you think he did with that?"

Paul shrugged and hoped that he looked interested as he didn't want to offend.

"He pushed the man under." The manager paused for effect "Because all that was visible was all that was left of the unfortunate chap."

Paul tried to feign incredulity at a tale he had heard from a number of sources. The same thing had happened at Round Oak when his father was a youth and at one of the smaller works of his grandfathers day. He had even read the story in a collection of short works set in Sheffield.

The tour went on and he was told of another event that had also taken place in Round Oak and possibly every other steelworks in the world. It was the one about the man who had gone into one of the empty furnaces which was a beautifully warm place for a sleep. No one had seen him go in and consequently no one knew he was in there when the furnace was fired up. Everyone of course heard his futile screams but by the time the furnace was again cool enough to enter there was not a trace left save the frantic scratch marks on the walls.

"That furnace has gone now but if we still had it I could have shown you the scratch marks on the brickwork."

Paul had been shown such scratch marks in a furnace at Round Oak by his father and wondered fleetingly whether scratch marks were a design feature of furnace walls to ensure that mythologies remained intact.

They had lunch in the managers canteen and were joined by a salesman and a young trainee manager. After the meal was over it was the latter who came out with a strange tale which he didn't want to recount while they were still eating.

"There's this woman who works with my mother and on Saturday she was going to the pictures with her boyfriend. They were a bit hungry so they went to the local fast food joint. They didn't open the packets until they got into the pictures. The boyfriend had chicken and he didn't think it tasted very nice so he left it. Had the shock of his life when the lights went up. Know what it was?..... A rat! Heaved his guts up he did. I think I would have done too."

The old manager took in the details. It was something shocking enough to be passed on. The tale made Paul feel uneasy, not on account of the content, but because he had heard exactly the same story told about someone visiting the pictures and the same fast food joint in Brierley Hill. The salesman began to laugh.

"I've heard that load of garbage in every town I've been to in the past fortnight."

The story teller's hackles rose. His integrity was in question.

"I'm not getting at you. I believed it first time I heard it. Why should I disbelieve it? But when the same tale is told in every town it's like saying that it happened in every town which makes me think it never happened at all. Something similar may have happened somewhere once and its been blown up and passed around as fact. It's a myth in short."

Paul felt like adding "Just like men falling into vats of molten steel or being locked in furnaces" but he refrained as he had his interview to consider which was that afternoon.

When he got home John asked how it had gone. Paul replied that it had been a day of myths but he was glad that people could still tell each other stories in the age of television. John didn't understand a word of the reply. He resumed watching the television. An advert came on proclaiming what an excellent company British Steel was these days. Good prospects because production was up. A government telling stories through the medium of television wasn't something to be so very happy about was the sentiment he expressed to his son. Paul knew exactly what his father was talking about.

HARRY CRAPPER

"Crapper!" the schoolkids would cry if they spotted his bent form in the town centre. The response never varied as Harry tore after the offending juveniles as fast as his short legs would carry him. Some kids only ventured "Harry!" which didn't always elicit a response. Even so, Harry Crapper must have been one of the fittest men in town as hardly a day went by without him pounding the town's pavements and, daily, hundreds of schoolkids had to use the central thoroughfares on their way home. During the war the army could find no use for him as he was declared unfit for service. He did persist however in trying to join the ranks with embarrassing regularity. "Not you again Crapper!" the recruiting sergeant would bawl.

The British Army having no use for Harry made one wonder if Harry was any use to anyone at all. He certainly looked perhaps a few bricks short of a load with a huge simple face, bulbous red nose, Hutchinson's teeth and gross halitosis. He could reek of sweat, not of honest endeavour, but of his insistence in wearing a heavy overcoat even on the hottest of summer days. He came over as a simpleton, a sort of latter day village idiot in an urban environment. Though he never did anything dishonest, Harry never did a days work in his life either so perhaps no one ever found a use for him, not even a liberal do-gooder could find a place for him beneath their protective wing.

Harry wouldn't have had a lot of use for a liberal do-gooder however in a world in which he made use of other people and things rather than the other way round. Harry's frequent visits to the army recruiting office had a great deal more to do with the enormous use he could have made of the British Army with it's bottomless pit of resources than any feelings of patriotism. Harry could doubtless have dealt those resources the sort of blow Hitler could only dream of. It wasn't to be but Harry learnt all the tricks. Dudley had scores of pubs and consequently scores of darts teams, crib teams and dominoes teams, all of whom had to be fed on match nights with the sandwiches their subscriptions had paid for. It was common practice for the food not consumed by the teams to be passed round the bar in which the match was played for the regular customers to avail themselves of the leftovers. Harry knew when every pub in town had its darts, crib and dominoes matches and his food bill was kept to a minimum by his practice of going from pub to pub and getting stuck into the food. Sometimes he would forget himself and get stuck in before the teams had had their's. It's no joke finishing a hard game of dominoes to find no food at the end of it and a highly satiated Harry Crapper looking down at empty sandwich plates. Not a lot could be said however because he couldn't be expected to take it in, he was doolally tap, the bloody army wouldn't have him and the army would have anyone.

Another common practice among many townies was to drink only halves as it was easier to be generous and for generosity to be reciprocated. Harry Crapper had down to a fine art his act of being a recipient of such generosity without ever having been known to reciprocate. As a result Harry's drinks bill never amounted to much if anything at all and he did drink a lot as he had he nose to prove it.

Harry's main source of income was the car parks which he worked on a regular basis. "Look after your car mate." Visitors to the town were unaware that the town's car parks were free and Harry did have the bearing of a car park attendant. Money for old rope. It nearly backfired one night when a visiting dignitary to the town hall said "Park it my good man." but Harry learnt to drive on the spot and exacted a fine tip.

His smokes were obtained by simple scrounging. "Got a fake mate?" If he spotted a stranger in a pub this direct approach coupled with simple persistence generally got him the cigarette he asked and a half pint.

Everyone in the town that kept him in food and drink knew him - simple bloke, used to sing "Red Tails in the Tuntet" in the Co-op office - and everyone at sometime or another must have found him a pain in the arse. He was a character however. Albeit a simple one, but a character nonetheless so he was held dear in people's hearts despite the occasional sham anger.

When he died in the early 1970s a notice in the local paper told how he left over £18,000, a lot of half pints in those days. A lot of people wondered how someone so "saft in the yed" could leave all that money.

My father folded the paper up and put it down.

"You know, I've worked all my life and then I look at Harry Crapper...... And I wonder who is bloody saft!"

* Based on a well known Dudley Character.

SHAFTED

Maurice, pronounced Moreece, was management, totally new to the game, college educated and not averse to making people aware of his superiority. Liaising with the foreman he insisted that the firm's best man be put on the job, he could shelve all his other tasks until this particular item was completed. The foreman led Maurice, pronounced Moreece, across the toolroom to Joe Jones, the company's most experienced and most adept man at the lathe. Maurice, pronounced Moreece, was going to tear the foreman off a strip as he wanted the company's best man, not its oldest but the foreman was adamant that Joe had few equals in the region and none in the company which could consider itself lucky to have him. The manager could have done without the foreman's lecture on the old engineers being a breed apart and loyalty being part of that breed but he allowed it to continue as he was anxious to return to his more natural habitat and he felt sure that the foreman would argue the point all day if he were to contradict. Once Joe had been pointed out as the man for the job Maurice, pronounced Moreece, went away and came back a few minutes later bearing a six foot shaft.

Joe looked the manager up and down and then studied the shaft from left to right before asking "What can I do for you gaffer?"

"I want you to make one of these for me," he said, studying Joe's face for a response.

The shaft was well worn in the middle from years of use and there were pits and grooves at either end from a bad fit in the machine from which it came. Joe pursed his lips.

"Well." Maurice, pronounced Moreece urged. "Can you do it?"

Joe studied the shaft again.

"You want me to mek a shaft like this one?"

"Yes, exactly like this one."

"Exactly like this one." Joe mused, almost to himself.

"Yes, exactly like this one." the manager confirmed.

"It'll tek time," Joe said eventually, "But I can't see there being any problems with it."

"Good. How long will it take?"

"A couple of days should see it through."

"Right, I want you to leave what you're doing and start on it straight away. I'll see you in a few days time."

Two days later Maurice, pronounced Moreece, descended on the tool room for his new shaft. Joe led him to the corner of the room and pulled away the sacking which covered the old and new shafts which lay side by side. Maurice, pronounced Moreece, blustered and burbled for a moment, went red in the face and looked decidedly unwell but no words would come.

Joe had turned the new manager a new shaft, exactly like the old one as ordered, complete with the wear in the middle and the pits and grooves at either end from the bad fit.

Maurice, pronounced Moreece, eventually spoke but it was to the foreman.

"You told me he was the best. He......He's an imbecile...Can't follow simple instructions....Two whole days work and a length of steel wasted by this....This fool. I'll see he gets his cards for this."

Joe looked at him evenly.

"Listen, Maurice. (Pronounced Maurice) There's a sign outside this works that says precision engineers. To be an engineer yoe have ter be precise. Yoe gie us summat ter mek an' we'll mek it, but only to the specifications we am gi'ed. Yoe asked for a shaft exactly like that un an' I med ya one. We tek orders son. We have to. It's up to yoe to gie out the right orders if yoe want to run an engineerin' works."

Maurice felt very much a Maurice after that. He quickly left the toolroom, well and truly shafted.

THE BREW'USS

It was not quite in the beginning, but it wasn't long after, that home-brew pubs abounded. Rakes of them there were. Had but a small fraction of them survived there would have been no need for any campaign for real ale, no cause célèbre for fell hikers, traction engine enthusiasts, folkies and followers of allied hobbies to sink their teeth into. The home-brew house was all but extinct by the early 1960s however and the nation was eventually inflicted with a campaign for real ale which supported real ale, real cider, real coal fires and proper bars - defined no doubt by the real rudeness any woman entering could expect.

The Brew'uss had been a home-brew pub until the late 1950s after which time the brewery at the back of the building stood derelict in the shadow of the town's biggest commercial brewing concern. Rumour had it that the Miller family who owned the Brew'uss never had a licence to brew but as they were right next door to a proper brewery no one could ever tell whether they were brewing or not. The decrepit building at the back certainly didn't look capable of brewing but folk used to like to think that the position of the pub itself allowed it to escape for so long the attentions of the people who inspect such things.

The sign outside was always pristine. The chronic air pollution never seemed to tarnish in any way the long board above the windows which read, "Miller's Free House & Home Brewed Ales". Just how the aforementioned inspectorate managed to miss the last part was a mystery. Perhaps they were meant to believe it was a joke. When brewing ceased it might well have been for the sign didn't change for a number of years. In fact not a lot did change as walking through the corridor from the street to the bar was like going down a time tunnel. The bar belonged to a different age. Blackout curtains hung at the windows. The paintwork was hidden beneath the dark brown nicotine staining of decades of quaffing smokers. The furniture was rude and elementary. A coal fire roared in the grate and the bar itself was a cross between an alehouse and a sweet shop as a glass cabinet filled with Mars bars, Bounties and Cadbury's Dairy Milk bars stood next to a jar filled with herbal tablets. One of the brothers used to hand the herbal tablets around the bar after having sawn them in half so as not to give too much away.

There were attempts to modernise, or at least keep up with the times, in the dim lit and decidedly dingy room. An inverted "Tupperware" box with a hole cut in the base served as a lampshade for one of the low Wattage bulbs which hung from the ceiling. Two cardboard cut-outs, one of the "Babycham" girl near the fire and one of the "Johnny Walker" man near the bar, added a splash of colour, and in the case of the former, a touch of feminine beauty to the bar. Being life sized, the figures often provided a listening ear to the bleary-eyed drunk, not that the Miller brothers tolerated drunks or bad language. An old car horn was sounded when a four letter word or profanity was uttered. Two toots of the horn for an individual meant being barred for life. A good many must have been barred for life for the only drinks which the Brew'uss sold in any quantity after its own brewery ceased activity were strong rot-brain cider and ginger beer. The former at least was a tongue loosener and the latter was certainly an accomplice as it was added as a splash to the cider to take off the tartness and hopefully reduce its evil effects. A bunch of seasoned drinkers from Leicester in town for a Baggies match, viewed as cissy the locals insistence on the splash of ginger beer. When joined by more of their townspeople the following evening they warned them to just have the splash however cissy or ridiculous it might sound.

The Brew'uss was filled with myth and mystery, the other-worldly aura made it inevitable. One thing for sure is that the brothers behind the bar were never seen to speak to one another. Although they lived under the same roof and ran a business together the firm belief was that they hadn't spoken to each other for over twenty years. The irrevocable difference was the result of some argument over a woman, or so the story goes.

Rumour had it that one of them was a talented concert pianist and the other had been in the merchant navy. The one who was supposed to have been a concert pianist certainly wore a bow tie whenever he was behind the bar which was nightly and the other appeared to have his sea legs. In the antediluvian lavatories he would have needed them, the plumbing hailing from two clear geological eras before the bar.

The Brew'uss was finally closed in the early 1980s amid much rumour and legend as to exactly when the closure would take place. An inspectorate other than the bootleg brewery one is said to have ordered the place closed on health and safety grounds. The story was that this had more to do with the health hazard of the primaeval urinals than any altruistic concern on the part of the inspectors for the safety of the clientele who consumed the cider. The absence of a campaign for real neolithic carsies meant that the doors of the Brew'uss were finally closed and access to the time tunnel was permanently barred.

The Brew'uss still stands and the sign above the windows is still in pristine condition six years after the closure. The the rumour now is that the brothers are refusing to fit new toilets. They are doubtless waiting for less than pristine sanitation to come back into fashion and with privatisation of water on the cards, the central government can't be blamed for not at least trying to accommodate them in seeing the health and safety obstacle removed and having the doors of the Brew'uss open once more to the public.

---

* Based on a Dudley pub, The Gypsies Tent. *The pub was legendary. This story reproduces some of the commonly held legends about the place. I have no doubt that there are many more in circulation. John Richards gives a comprehensive account of the facts in "The Pubs & Breweries of the Old Dudley Borough".*

THE COUNTRY PUB

Dad may have come across it in his cycling days before the war. It was certainly out of the way lying well off the beaten track somewhere between Bridgnorth and Claverley. It was one of those balmy summer evenings when it remains light until late on. The family were progressing, sister was out courting so there were just the four of us; Mom, Dad, Butch the dog and me. The Severn valley was a well used evening retreat for Black Country people in the summer and we had been over the river for a walk around Bridgnorth. The journey back was an easy meander through the lanes around Claverley. The intention was to call in for a drink there but the sight of *The Red Lion O' Morfe* on the left made Dad pull into the side to take a look.

"I thought there was a pub around here," he said.

A signpost over the lane read "Upper Farmcote", the name of the hamlet which comprised *The Red Lion O' Morfe*, the house next door, the barn at the back, a few cottages a quarter of a mile up the lane, a telegraph pole and the sign itself. Upper Farmcote, or Morfe, was, according to the sign, two miles from Claverley and three from Heathton.

It had to be a real McCoy country pub as it wasn't mobbed with thirsty Black Country folk on a night out. There were a few rustics about but not enough to make it a hive of activity. We sat outside in the warm still evening. Men were coming in occasionally, straight from the field.

Now Butch was a scrapper who would have a go at anything that moved. The old farmer and his toothless dog coming up the path didn't send our pulses racing when Butch went to challenge the aging canine. What exactly happened we were never able to fathom but it was one of the few fights that Butch lost in his illustrious career and he lost it before we had chance to call him back from the path.

Not many minutes afterwards we had finished our drinks and were on the way back to Dudley. I never thought of remembering the route home, I wasn't at that sort of age.

Two years later I was at an age when pubs meant a bit more than crisps and Vimto. Sister was about to be married and I had just left school. It was summer and a favourite pastime was heading out to the country to our haunts which had already become regular. *The Queen's Head* in the eerie village of Wolverley, Kinver's well laden High Street, *The Six Ashes* in the village of the same name, and of course *The Cider House* where the tax had yet to make an impact and a pint was only ten pence. Mac and I were out on a Saturday night drive to nowhere in particular. We were well into clocking up new country pubs and I had spoken of *The Red Lion* out Claverley way but I wasn't sure of its exact location. As a secluded country pub, finding it had become something of a quest with us though our searches had been to no avail. Somewhere out near Pattingham we got involved in a car chase with another couple of shavers that took us down the narrowest of country lanes and even across a farmyard. After quite a hectic and hair-raising spell which took us a good few miles the pursuing car signalled that the race was over and a good time had been had by all. Mac turned left out of a narrow lane away from Claverley which was about a mile distant. We hadn't travelled far when, as if by magic, *The Red Lion O' Morfe* appeared on our right.

Again there didn't seem many people about, a few cars outside - no car park as such, just a bit of space in between the house and the pub which led to a track into the fields. Mac pulled into that space alongside an old Bentley. One of the other cars was a 1960s Alfa Romeo. The rest were the standard models of the day but to have two distinctive cars among so few gave the senses a refreshing tingle of excitement extra to that of actually having found the place. There were one or two people outside drinking pints, their shirts undone halfway down their chests which were ruddied through working in the fields. They watched us as we got out of the car and walked into the pub, townies were an exception. Through the front door the rear of a high-backed settle to the right gave the impression of a corridor. A door to the left led to a small lounge. The semi-circular bar lay past the settle. At the bar we could view the room; the settle, a few benches, old tables and stools. There was an open fireplace on one wall. Above it were two paintings of the same boy; in one he was keen to smoke a pipe, in the other he was ill from the experience of smoking it. There was another painting of a very early railway with some men frantically trying to pull a stubborn mule across the line before the train arrived. There were a number of framed photographs of Victorian politicians and military men as well as a few views of Shropshire. There were two old ladies behind the bar, sisters by the look of them.

"Evening lads," they said in a Shropshire accent. "What can we get you?"

Mac ordered a Newcastle Brown Ale and I a Newcastle Amber. While pouring them one of the women noted, "From Dudley baint you?"

We nodded, somewhat bowled over by the hospitality and the fact that our home town had been detected by the way we spoke. To our chagrin we were usually called Brummies.

In the room were a number of characters. We tried to place them to the cars outside. A huge Orson Welles figure with a curly moustache and goatee beard dressed in a black jacket and grey trousers wore pince-nez and looked very much the country squire. To him we assigned the Bentley as he was the first person with the bearing of a Bentley driver we had *ever* seen in the flesh. He stood with a shorts glass in his hand surveying the room with an air of distinction. People seemed to treat him with deference. At one of the tables sat a couple. To them, we felt, the Alfa Romeo belonged. The woman was black-haired with piercing brown eyes and Mediterranean features. Her clothes were expensive looking but not new, her jewelry ostentatious. She could easily have been mistaken for Sophia Loren. The man wore one of the new style suits that African politicians had made popular, the jacket loose fitting with more pockets than enough. With a balding pate and sinister expression he looked a bit like the Master, Doctor Who's arch foe. While the squire looked at home in the bar, the couple looked a shade incongruous as the remainder of the clientele were farmhands.

Jack was corpulent and ruddy. His Shropshire accent, though thick, was understandable to us. The old Paul had bronzed aquiline features. His swift beady eyes gave the impression of alertness but the cap perched way back on his forehead lent a comic appearance which his short stature and bandy legs compounded. His speech was thoroughly incomprehensible to us though everyone else seemed to understand him. The young Paul was big and blithe with a simple face. He looked strong enough to tackle anyone. He seemed to pay us no mind.

It was a strange feeling being in a country pub unspoilt by town people. To be viewing something first hand lent an air of excitement but there went with it constant reminders that we had seen it all before on the television. The farmhands were all that the small screen had taught us to expect. In the days before talk of stereotypes, they seemed to have got their stereotypes right. Funnily enough, if we were to have put a label on the incongruous couple it would have had film or television people written on it.

It may have been down to a touch of culture shock, but we only had one drink before returning to Dudley with a feeling of having visited another world. In the coming days our friends were to hear of the experience.

The following week the cultural exchange was even greater. Mac came along, I was accompanied by Anne, then there was Bob and Lenny. The two old ladies behind the bar recognised us and poured our Newcastle Brown and Newcastle Amber while the others deliberated. The characters from the previous Saturday were in. This time they eyed us with suspicion.

Jack went outside and we heard him say, "Ere, there be a blackie in the bar."

No one was offended, it wasn't a malicious comment. The pub was relatively untouched and all of us were foreigners. We sort of got on well that night mutually making fun of each other without going over the top.

The way we spoke was a source of amusement to them. The young Paul held court about rooting. I think he had his eye on Anne.

"Ere, I bin rootin' all over the world. I bin rootin' in Wellington. Not Wellington Shropshire, Wellington New Zealand."

There followed some banter about penis size which they related to farm animals.

"E be pig's cockee."

"I baint. I be got horse's cockee."

Like the room, its decor and the characters in it, the conversation took on an air of unreality. It was a night that would be recalled for many a year.

We visited the pub a number of times that summer and felt able to nod "how do?" to the young Paul and pass the time of day with Jack and the old Paul. Sometimes if Lenny wasn't with us they'd ask "when be you bringing the blackie down again. He be a laugh." The squire character remained aloof and we felt the couple to be beyond our social capabilities.

The following spring we drove out that way again as soon as the weather broke. There were fairy lights outside, a mass of cars, Black Country accents everywhere. The old ladies were gone from behind the bar, a man from Brierley Hill had taken it over. He kept a good house and it continued to be a good night out. The characters were still there. However, they were swamped in a sea of that with which we were familiar. We still enjoyed the place yet felt sad at the passing of the old pub of which we had caught a fleeting glimpse. We also felt privileged in that we had seen a timeless country pub in its last summer.

PLAYING AWAY

All the fuss was quite staggering really. Real Ale was making a come back. Glossy magazines and colour supplements carried articles about the consumer action group that had succeeded in halting the tide of bland gassy beer that had flooded the country at the expense of the living liquid. All power to their elbow Karl Houseman thought but as far as he was concerned real ale had never been away. His home town of Dudley, within the boundaries of its extended Metropolitan Borough, had five breweries: Hansons brewery in the town centre, the Dudley part of Wolverhampton and Dudley breweries; Batham's in Brierley Hill with eight pubs; Simpkiss, also in Brierley Hill, with sixteen pubs; Holdens in Woodsetton with around a dozen pubs; and old Ma Pardoes in Netherton with the brewery at the back of the pub, the speak your weight machine in the bar and scarcely room to swing a cat in the snug, one of the flagships of the real ale movement. People came on pilgrimages from all over the country to Pardoes where they would look agog at the enamel ceiling and the stove in the middle of the room, take photographs of the exterior, talk loudly of all the other interesting pubs they'd visited in places no one has ever heard of, hold the beer up to the light, dip litmus paper in it, talk about it with a knowledgeable air at great length - anything but drink the stuff. Yes, Karl knew all about real ale and its aficionados and viewed them with a sort of detached amusement.

In the early days he had seen the good beer guide as a good idea for the unsuspecting boozer on a trip to places like London or Cornwall, but not for folk in the Black Country who knew where everything was anyway. Dudley itself had so few pubs in the guide and those that were were all around the bus station. CAMRA must have sent someone in by bus who could have tarried no further than a hundred yards from the bus stop so Karl knew the guide to be a waste of time for his home town but he had faith in the selection of pubs in the beer deserts of the south. Until he put the theory to the test that is. *The Chainlocker* in Falmouth, an harbourside pub with a drop of good material on tap by all accounts. What was missing from those accounts was that the beer tasted like it had been pumped directly out of the old harbour. After that experience the guide was something of a joke to Karl who either trusted his luck on sorties away from home or drank lager. The movement grew despite the absence of Karl from its ranks and real ale came into fashion.

It was in the early 1980s that Karl found himself in a West End tavern with an hour or so to kill before catching the train north. It was a while since he had been in London and much to his surprise there was on the bar a majestic old beer pull. Without thinking he ordered a pint of bitter and was served up some gassy soapy sort-of beer. He felt obliged to drink it, which he did with great alacrity so that he could sample the draught bitter. "Bitter please" he said. "This one." pointing to the beer pull. "Oh, you mean 'Snowcrocks Old and Detestable'" the barman said with a great deal of condescension in his delivery. Real ale was the fashion in the city, the uninitiated from the sticks had to be put in their place when it came to purchasing it. Karl viewed the barman disdainfully but also with the relish that his knowledge of the subject was infinitely superior to the young man's should he labour the point.

About a month later Karl again found himself in London with all his business completed before lunchtime. He roamed the West End pubs forearmed with the knowledge that real ale was the "in" thing with the city gent and the executive type. Five to three saw him in *The Cambridge* on Cambridge Circus. He had had a few prior to entering and it probably showed in that by then he didn't particularly care. The floor was covered with a thin smattering of sawdust and in the corner a blind guitarist perched precariously on a stool crooned John Denver songs. Two city looking stereotypes in pinstripe suits sipped at pints of flat beer between conversation in old Etonian tones. They watched Karl as his eyes scanned the beer pulls for the choice available.

Among the array of pumps one was for Fosters, the Australian lager. Now Karl had never seen Fosters on tap before. He had drunk it out of tins that look more suited to containing motor oil but he had never seen, let alone sampled, the draught version. He was also of the sort of disposition whereby he would try anything once, especially after six pints of grog. He duly ordered a pint of Fosters.

Karl must have looked a decent sort of chap that day. Obviously not one of the landed gentry but a decent sort nonetheless, a chap deserving of a touch of good fortune. One of the old Etonians came to Karl's assistance, chiming up, "I say old boy. That's lager!"

Karl turned round and blearily faced his benefactors.

"Ar, ah know" he said. "I'm from Dudley" he added as though that was all that needed to be said on the matter. The gentlemen of the city at least took the information as though it was.

THE BLUE TEAPOT

Aunt Ada busied herself in the kitchen. There was bread to be buttered, sandwiches to be made and, above all, tea to be brewed. Outside the sun shone brilliantly and she had hoped not to say to anyone that it was a good day for it but almost everyone who had arrived so far had shrugged shoulders and said "Ah well, at least it's a good day for it." Funerals weren't supposed to be good, they were meant to be bad days, sad days, but they were family occasions and it was true, there was no point in wishing for gloomy weather to add to the despondency pervading the household. So why not admit to it, it was a good day for it.

Ada didn't care much for funerals. At an early age she discovered that they upset her terribly and as a consequence went to great lengths to ensure that the only one she would attend would be her own. Local tradition went some way to keeping Ada and funerals well apart in that women folk weren't obliged to "follow" and in some cases weren't expected to follow even their own husband's funeral. Ada's nephew Garry worried her on this score. He didn't seem to be a party to the old values as he got most irate by people who asked him if his mother was going to follow his father's funeral. To Garry the question was preposterous, how could a wife not go to her own husband's funeral. To the poser of the question it was a fair point for contingent on the reply was whether they would have to take their own wife along. Unfortunately for Ada, her sister in law Winnie didn't hold much with the old ways either. There was no question of her not following which meant that Ada too might be expected to go. It was after all her own brother who was to be sent to meet his maker - officially that is as money had already changed hands over the proposition that he would have done a few games of dominoes with his new landlord by the end of the first night.

Someone was always required, however, to stay behind and make the tea ready for the family's return from the cemetery, or in this case the crematorium. It was usually a neighbour who undertook that task and Mrs Ranu from next door had been gratefully accepted to the post before Ada had had a chance to get a look in. She volunteered nonetheless and though she was quite unaware of the fact, her dislike of funerals was common knowledge and it was agreed that she help Mrs Ranu in the catering department for the morning.

A number of things troubled Ada. It was as though something was lacking in Garry's upbringing. He obviously wasn't a party to things it was right for a young man of his age to know. Sister in law Winnie and her dear departed brother in their liberal approach had overlooked some of the time honoured essentials of life. She would obviously have to play some part in Garry's enlightenment herself as it was too late for his father to do so and Winnie wouldn't be in any position to, what with losing her husband and everything.

Garry entered the kitchen expecting a scowl. It was no place for a man on the morning of a funeral. Everything seemed to have a pattern. He could see that and it appealed to him, for while he was sympathetic to feminism, it did in his view lack a certain grace. He was surprised at his Aunt Ada's reception of him into her domain. She called him over and he at once had the feeling that he was to be told something important. The lid on the electric kettle rattled while on the stove an old whistling kettle began to chirp merrily. Ada turned down the gas and began.

"Now then, that there is the family teapot." Garry took in the large cream enamel teapot which stood on the stove next to the whistling kettle. It had a green rim and a triangular chip the size of a sixpence out of the lid.

"It holds sixteen cups of tea and it belongs to all the family. If you have any parties its yours to use as much as anybody's. I'm the one who keeps it at the minute. I don't know who it will pass to when I go but if you have a party, you only have to ask and its there to be used."

Garry was expecting her to add that 28 days notice in writing was required plus a cogent reason but Ada's little edifying speech ended there. He certainly felt as though he had been made party to a snippet of sacred knowledge and Ada for her part felt that she had got her message across well and had done the family duty.

Garry was on his way out of the kitchen without the cup of tea he had gone in for when he was called back. Now Ada didn't have it in her to be prejudiced but she did appreciate that her understanding could be a little lacking.

"One other thing. Mrs Ranu..."

"Yes she'll be along as soon as we've gone to the service. She didn't want to encroach on family affairs even though she's more than welcome in this house any time."

It wasn't what Ada wanted to know. She felt silly for asking but she had called Garry back now. "She's alright with tea isn't she?" Ada whispered.

"Expert!" Garry reassured her. "She's catering manager at Coates canteen."

He again left without a cup of tea but Ada was happy that she had sorted that out. She didn't want to put her foot in it and it had been such a good day up until then. With the worry about the catering removed she got to thinking that maybe the other members of the family of Garry's age should learn things as well.

While everyone was away Ada and Mrs Ranu prepared the buffet. Just before the family returned Mrs Ranu went home, not wanting to gate-crash the family occasion. Ada's persuasive powers for once failed her as even she couldn't get her brother's good neighbour to stay. The buffet was consumed and the family teapot played a major role in keeping everyone plied with tea. It didn't make social appearances very often but when it did it could always be relied upon to give a good performance. Ada was pleased with the way things had gone.

A number of people had paid their respects and gone so the house was starting to empty and there were free seats. Ada couldn't sit down however as it was time to start clearing away. The men folk thought they would aid the process by getting from under the women's feet. The best way of doing this would be to get out of the house altogether which they did and so as not to appear an unruly mob of ne'er do wells on a street corner, ensconced themselves in the nearest public house.

The women cleared away and when the men returned it was time for another cup of tea.

Ada's cousin Frank, who had been silent for most of the day seemed to wake up from out of his dreams.

"Whatever happened to the blue teapot?" he asked the assembly in general.

All the older people present seemed to know exactly what Frank was talking about but equally no one seemed to know exactly whereabouts it was.

The younger generation were a bit agog at the news that there was, somewhere within the family, a blue teapot. Ada had been round them all in the morning and explained the existence and purpose of the family teapot. So, they had started the day, in family terms, as teapot-free persons. Now they had two! It was all a bit much to take in.

The blue teapot had belonged to their great grandparents and had been passed down the line. Everyone remembered it but no one had seen it for twenty five years. There was much discussions as to where it might be but the favourite theory was that great Aunt Clarrissa who had moved through marriage up to Manchester had taken it with her.

The younger generation had learnt quickly, despite being unaware for so long, of the importance of teapots within the family. Now the family teapot was in Ada's keeping and was theirs to have and to hold tea whenever they so desired but the mysterious blue teapot being missing and possibly in Manchester was something they weren't prepared to accept lightly. Two plans were discussed. One was to invade Manchester and conduct a house to house search. The other was to find where this

Clarrissa had moved to and go and steal it. The search for the blue teapot was on.

There were a number of family occasions over the next two years, a wedding, a christening, a retirement party, but no clues were forthcoming as to the whereabouts of the blue teapot. Much to everyone's surprise Garry, the perennial bachelor, announced his engagement on his late father's birthday in December. The wedding was to be the following July, a long time away that rolled around like it was five minutes.

At the reception everyone seemed jovial. Much alcohol had been consumed by the time the coffee was served and as coffee is also served from pots the conversation got round to teapots. Uncle Bill was the oldest brother and had lived a bit out on a limb near Wolverhampton. The fuss about teapots was beyond him but he did feel obliged to mention that he had one in his possession.

The top table noticed the general excitement from the ranks which culminated in Aunt Ada standing up and shouting to the assembly.

"We've fun [found] the blue taypot!"

Most of the guests were bemused by this. The best man explained to his wife who was from Devon clearly, one syllable at a time.

"They have fun the blue tay pot." as though it was simplicity itself.

It turned out that the mysterious blue teapot had been at the bottom of Bill's wardrobe for twenty five years which was where he put it on the day that Frank had given it to him.

Bill returned to the evening party with the blue teapot in his possession. It was placed behind the bar for all to see.

Horace has the blue teapot now. She, yes she, went to have it priced at a valuers. It is over a hundred years old and entirely valueless. She put it in the sink with a view to washing it one time but then decided against such an action in case any of the blue came off. A blue teapot that wasn't blue would have been no good for use nor ornament.

THE GLORIOUS REVOLUTION

It was long ago, in his youth, that it had struck him; the perfect likeness of bourgeois elitism as displayed by the British middle class and democratic centralism as displayed by comrade Lenin. It was in a lounge bar of a lunchtime in the age of Thatcher. The lounge was filled with young business types, the monotonously dull Yuppies for whom the Thatcher years were a continual lunchtime. It had always amused him to listen to people who were reaping the rewards of the new paper prosperity. They liked to talk about democracy. Democracy was implicitly good and implicitly free. Real fighters for freedom they were when expounding their views on democracy. One group were entertaining a paid officer of the local housing department, a high ranking one too. Some place in the conversation, it slipped out, between the astounding revelation that if one made ones phone calls during office hours one got more business done and a graphic description of the assumed insatiable sexual appetite of one of the secretaries - gleaned from the cut of her clothes. Quite obscure at first but then the gist became clear. They had just won a contract from the local authority. Through the paid officer they could provide a "neat package". Of course for a few awkward weeks it looked as though the councillors would put the business elsewhere, not at all what the paid officer wanted. Had to be guided these councillors, like children they were. Local authorities had to be run, could only be run, by the professional class. Things couldn't be left to the democratically elected representatives of the citizens. Quite novel he had thought until his brain threw back at him violently. THAT'S STRAIGHT LENINISM. A professional elite to guide the people down the right path.... But they weren't communists, these were the dynamos of British Capitalism, the manager class. Either way, the people of a nation: they couldn't organise a piss up in a brewery if left to do it on their own. But that was then, way back.

Rodney Tumeley had been hammering out chains by an age old method ever since his Y.T.S. landed him in the sunrise heritage industry. Nationalisation had long been an evil. Government investment where private investment was lacking was never a way of looking at things - except among the so called loony left. Privatisation was the flavour of the era. The huge loss making giants were sold off one by one following expensive propaganda with the message to private investors that here indeed were some tasty and profitable morsels. The average Briton would be a home owning share owning democrat. Meanwhile the government of privatisation and freedom invested millions in the nationalisation of unemployment to bring the figures down while they expended much energy in silencing opposition and reducing freedom of speech. Rodney was lucky, his two years conscription in a nationalised industry gave him a genuine skill, albeit a very archaic one, and even a real job.

When Rodney started out in his working life the only heavy engineering that the government had any interest in was called social, social engineering. The old manufacturing industries which required huge capital investment to finance and vast retinues of workers to run were removed from Britain's landscape piecemeal. Steel, coal, ship building. Thousands of workers who could organise and have a say in where the capital fuelling their industry went all of a sudden went themselves. It wasn't so much the destruction of the industries that was important but the destruction of the unions, the thorns in the flesh of the British capitalist for over a century. A new servant class was created in the process and they would be needed for the capitalists were doing alright. Manufacturing industries were gravitating towards the Pacific rim which was fine by them because the City of London was vital to the worlds financial system. And millions of new jobs were created in Britain too supplementary to nationalised unemployment. All shopping malls and leisure complexes and heritage museums had to be staffed under the oppression of the Trade Union Movement. The lower wages and the no strike agreements. The non union labour and the disregard for employees rights. It was heaven!

It was a dark star that rose in the east however. A certain proportion of the British might have become stinkingly rich on paper money and noughts on computers but once a steel works has been bulldozed it can no longer produce steel, a flattened ship yard can launch absolutely nothing. Over the years Britain's capability to produce its own wealth was eroded to nothing. The shops and leisure parks certainly didn't produce any though they did make a tidy profit for their owners who saw that this was good. Meanwhile the inscrutable folk of the far east produced an increasing proportion of the worlds wealth. One day, it literally happened overnight, it was realised that the City of London wasn't actually required for anything and so the plug was pulled. All the noughts went off the screens and all the paper was worthless and lo, Britain was finished as the only thing it made was chains and the like in the heritage museums. Rodney wasn't really into Marx but he had the historical nouse to realise that he was, with a few hundred others, the industrial proletariat, never mind the vanguard.

After the stock market was switched off, there was nothing so grand as a crash, Britain's capitalists had a hard time of it. However, with the new affluent workers being out on the Pacific some far sighted people developed the notion that they might anker after the roots of the toils in which they were now engaged. Shakespeare country had to play second fiddle to the Black Country. England was the place for an exotic holiday for the newly rich oriental. That was the sales pitch at any rate. Luckily for Britons, it worked and the punters flocked in from the far east in their thousands every year, and in a new sort of way, Britain prospered. Rather the old ruling classes worked things so that they prospered far better than the man in the museum. Rodney watched it all with amusement. Never a red or anything like that, the passing of the great opportunity of the British people to kick their rulers into touch once and for all had to be laughed at for even the rulers themselves couldn't believe it when they came out of the crisis with their power intact. And I'm the proletariat he thought, quite often without realising how powerful he was - in a revolutionary sense. A young student of politics once quipped "I wonder whatever happened to the proletariat?" To which his friend replied "He's over there." Rodney was taking a breather from his hammering at the time so he heard the joke. It was then that it came to him. If he was to unite with the other museum artisans then he would indeed have nothing to lose but his chains.

With the powers that be remaining the powers that be, they assumed that their right to treat people how they pleased remained unchanged so they went into the glorious revolution in such a position of overwhelming superiority that it wasn't even designated a minor industrial dispute. It was May Day that Rodney did it, he could have acted at Easter but Monday May 7th, which was May Day Bank Holiday that year seemed a more symbolic day for a revolution. It was a glorious day weather wise so the museum was expecting bumper crowds. The chain shop was a major attraction which was good for business as the punters worked up a sweat watching the action and the first thing they clapped eyes on once out of the workshop was the pub, the real Victorian shipped brick by brick from Brierly Hill spit sawdust and real ale pub - with up to the minute prices. Not that that seemed to deter anyone as the pub did better than the chain shop in that no one actually bought any chains but barrels of beer were consumed daily.

The pub opened early and a handful of professional drinkers cheerfully sniffed it out. Rodney took a stool near the bar, bought a pint, and waited. It wasn't long before the lack of a man making chains was noticed as visitors arrived to consume the museum's menu of canal barges old shops and houses, coal mines, chapels and cars. A party of Korean chain forgers were most put out and demanded to see the manager who sympathised and grew steadily hotter under the collar as he thought about the absence of his chain maker. There weren't many blue collar workers left to push around, in fact Rodney was the only one he knew, so he would enjoy tearing him off a strip, whatever the excuse was for his lateness. He apologised to the Koreans and explained that the chain shop would be open for performances later on in the day. He had a subordinate put up a notice to that effect and bellowed over the loudspeaker, "Will Rodney Tumeley report to the chain shop immediately!" A guide book seller was stationed outside the chain shop and she was to report to the manager the moment Rodney returned.

Inside the pub the bar was filling up. The laughter and chatter muffled the announcement so that it wasn't heard. The gaffer of the pub was what would have been called a working class Tory in the days when there was a working class but as there wasn't he was just a plain obnoxious self centred cuss.

"No chains today?" he said to Rodney when he served him.

Rodney said nothing. He shook his head to indicate the negative. 'No chains no never no more', he was thinking.

The population of the bar doubled with the arrival of the Korean chain makers. The gaffers face beamed. His mind was counting the days takings already. The bar staff sweated to serve the rush while he sauntered about keeping an eye on things. He came from behind the bar to open one of the windows fully. After catching snatches of conversation in broken English about the chain shop he quizzed Rodney on the way back.

"I thought you said the chain shop was shut today?"

"It is gaffer, it is." Rodney replied. It was his turn to beam. His hour was coming.

The gaffer didn't like the supercilious nature of the reply and coupled with the fact that he didn't believe Rodney in the first instance that the chain shop would be closed on a bank holiday, he became very suspicious. Outside a second announcement bellowed round the museum.

"Will Rodney Tumeley report to the chain shop immediately!"

The museum manager had sent someone round to Rodney's house who on finding it empty had reported back. The manager too was suspicious as he had been brought up not to like Rodney's sort. He was up to something, the manager was sure, but whatever it was would be dealt with summarily. Decades of pent up anger at the working class with no working class to vent it on were welled up inside him. The hour was approaching when he could get his own back.

The gaffer was taken back by the effrontery of it all. The chain maker had totally ignored the command and the only action he had taken immediately was to order a fresh pint. His first impulse was to take the pint away, frogmarch Rodney down to the chain shop and then sack on the spot the barperson who had served him. His second thought was that the barperson concerned was his wife and that sacking her might not be politic. His third thought, which was sobered by the second, was much better. He would have some entertainment. He rubbed his hands gleefully and picked up the phone.

The gaffer positioned himself for a good view. Through the window he could see the manager, red faced, come storming towards the pub. The doors burst open and the scene was set for the opening salvos of the glorious revolution. The Koreans and the other patrons had stopped in their tracks after the dramatic entrance. Rodney however remained on the bar stool with his back to the door supping his pint with theatrical arrogance.

"Tumeley!" the manager bawled. "To the chain shop." He paused for a while so that he could shout "Immediately!" after a Rodney who was already on his way. The trouble was that Rodney remained on his bar stool. Deliberately finishing his pint and putting the glass down before turning round slowly to face the manager. "Are you addressing me?"

This threw the manager as it didn't altogether fit in with the script as he had imagined it. He grew hotter under the collar as he fumbled for the right words. He eventually found them.

"What is the meaning of this" he glowered. "Insubordination." He would have gone on to fire Rodney on the spot and have him removed from the museum never to return but the chain maker got in first.

"I've had a basinful." he spat. His anger was much more controlled. "Low wages, filthy conditions while you lord it over us....er....me."

"In the good old days, if the 'workers' hadn't used to like it they were always free to go elsewhere. And now, you will go elsewhere. You're fired."

Rodney was quite alarmed. This was the glorious revolution and *he* was the only shot that had been fired. He picked up the stool and hurled it at the window but the window had been opened fully and it flew outside where it hit a passer-by.

"Viva la revolution!" he shouted.

The English stared in amazement while the Koreans grinned and applauded, thinking it to be part of some natural theatre played out every day to give visitors a taste of how work shy the British were.

Two young men entered. One of them was carrying a bar stool in such a way as to suggest that he might use it on Rodney in the same manner as the chain maker had hoped to use it on the window.

"Call the police" the manager instructed the gaffer before trying to placate the injured party with a "Now now no violence please gentlemen", even though the injured man and his pal looked quite unlike the sort of people he would normally refer to as gentlemen.

"This man has gone mad. We are calling the police to have him removed."

Rodney couldn't wait for the police to come so that he could be dragged away screaming "Viva la revolution" and suchlike. The revolution was failing. What's more, the men didn't seem to want to wait for due process to run its course before justice was served. Enforcing their own seemed much more likely as they, together with the stool, faced rodney. At this high point in the drama about half a dozen flash bulbs went off simultaneously as the Koreans took photographs for posterity. The players were blinded for a few seconds but as the effects wore off Rodney recognised the young man brandishing the stool. It was the student who had made the quip about the proletariat.

"Which side are you on boys, this is the glorious revolution!" he shouted.

About this time the two young men realised who it was they were about to batter.

"It's the proletariat" the one said.

"The revolutionary proletariat" the other one corrected as he put down the stool.

Four policemen burst in. The manager shouted "There he his, arrest that man before there is blood spilt." But the face off was over as the two men were exchanging fraternal greetings with Rodney.

"We're with you all the way comrade!"

"Do you want your stool back?"

After a lot of questioning the police decided that the only crime that had been even vaguely committed was the manager wasting their time. They lectured him severely but didn't press charges.

Rodney was sacked and there was no going back on that but the gaffer of the pub had changed allegiances. Sacking a man was one thing, having him arrested for throwing a stool at a student was another. It was the gaffer therefore who pointed out that Rodney had paid to get into the museum that morning and was therefore a bona fide customer and therefore could not be thrown out just because he had been sacked and as for the affray, well , the police themselves had pointed out that there were no charges to answer. That put an effective end to the glorious part of Rodney's revolution, there were no symbolic scenes either in his case or in museums up and down the country where the proletariat struck its blow at the heart of British rulers.

The museum managers were first to feel the effects. Rodney's manager had put the Koreans off until the afternoon and indeed they were well-pleased with the entertainment in the pub but a stream of people saw him throughout the day complaining of the number of miles they had come to see a real chain shop in action. At first the manager wasn't worried. Had there not been an age of transferable skills. Could not the tram driver sell ice cream as well as drive trams. Could not the bargee sell programmes as well as do canal trips. Despite a host of staff on the books with equally wide ranging skills, there was not one to be found who could make chains as well as sell ice cream. This problem repeated itself throughout the land. The attraction of the museums diminished. Less beer and ice cream was sold. Jobs were lost and Britain again started slipping down down down. There were people with the skills but they just weren't in the right places. That was the argument of the rulers. Britain was once more on the verge of collapsing and no one seemed to know why.

Meanwhile the proletariat weren't worried, nor were they engaged in subversive activities. Most of them got jobs as vendors of some description. At least it was a job. It would do until the lights went out.

CHRISTMAS CARD TO LEV

1) *Halcyon Days:*

Karl Houseman was a Baggie; a supporter of West Bromwich Albion Football Club. Most of his social circle were "Wolves blokes"; supporters of the Baggies' great Black Country rivals Wolverhampton Wanderers. Now loyalties were one thing, facts were another. In a run that lasted from resumption of the professional game after the war right through till the early 1960s Wolves had been the "top club in the land". Karl knew Bert Bartlett's monologue by heart; he had heard it often enough. The bar was full and Bert was holding court.

"Three times Football League Champions; 1954, 1958 and 1959. Three times runners up; 1950, 1955 and 1960. Four times third place; 1947, 1953, 1956 and 1961. Twice winners of the F.A. Cup; 1949 and 1960; semi-finalists in 1951." "Nobody could touch them...."

Bert had developed his piece over the years. He knew all the counter arguments and he was no bigot so he incorporated them into his monologue with due deference to the other great teams and players of the 1950s.

"And before you say it; Manchester United. Three Championships in the same period. Two F.A. Cup wins, twice beaten finalists too. But still not the sustained occupation of the top three places as the Wolves. And yes I know about the Munich air disaster...."

There was always a silence at this point, a mark of respect for the loss British football suffered. Bert would digress.

"The finest footballer ever.... and he came from Dudley, from off the Priory...." Bert would always cast a glance about his audience at this stage. The "know who he was?" was an optional addition if a younger face presented.

"Duncan Edwards. And he played in a great side, the Busby Babes.

"There were a lot of good sides about in the 'fifties. Newcastle, Jackie Milburn. Won the cup three times. Blackpool. Stanley Matthews. One cup win and two finals after the war. The Baggies had a good side too. But the Wolves were the best of the lot...."

Karl knew "the finest sides in Europe" bit came next. His glass as empty so he went to the bar reciting it to himself.

We had them all down at the Molineux. Ferencvaros, Honved. Puskas came with Honved. And Moscow Dynamo. Now that for me was the greatest match. Lev Yashin was their captain. The greatest goalkeeper in the world before Gordon Banks took the crown. He was a showman, Yashin, used to joke with the crowd. They loved him down the Molineux.

I'll never forget him. 9th of November 1955. 55,840 on the ground, most ever for a friendly. Old Yashin kept us entertained. Couldn't keep the ball out of the net though. 2-1 to Wolves in the finish...."

Karl returned to Bill's table in time to recant in unison.

"Bill Slater in the 14th minute, Jimmy Mullen in the 49th and Illyn pulled one back for them."

The whole company joined in to shout the closing line of the monologue.

"Ar. Them was the halcyon days."

2) The Plan

It was Saturday lunchtime. Bill sat in the bay window in the bar of *The Light* in Dudley. He was studying form. Karl sat on a stool at right angles to the bar. He was studying the morning paper too.

Karl was a football generation younger than Bill. The younger often pulled the leg of the older. The question "what was the name of that goalie yoe used to like Bill? The Russian at the Wolves?" set Bill up to expect a gag.

Yashin was not that remote from Karl however. He remembered him in his last World Cup in 1966.

It was with a sense of shock and a tinge of sadness that Karl read the filler.

"Lev Yashin, once considered the greatest goalkeeper in the world, is dying of cancer in a Moscow hospital." That was all it said.

Karl called Bill over to the bar. "Come and have a look at this."

Bill scanned the few lines. "It's like nobody cares" was all he said.

The rest of the lunchtime session was spent in silence. Karl read the rest of his paper only looking up to sip his beer. Bill, for the most part, stared at the pint he never finished.

That evening Bill was in early. Or it could have been Karl was in late. Bill had recovered his composure. Many of the heroes of his youth had already passed away. Lev Yashin was still in the land of the living. On his way out, yes; but still in the land of the living.

Bill had told all the crew, many of whom had been on the Molineux on that November day in 1955, of Lev Yashin lying, dying in a Moscow cancer ward. When Karl walked in one of them told him about it.

Bill put the record straight. "Ar, it was Karl as told me."

One of the less sporting tried to put in a jibe about Karl supporting the Baggies and being beyond caring as a consequence. Karl cut short the rancour. From his pocket he produced a Christmas card with explanation that it would be sent by the football supporters of the west midlands. Everyone agreed it would be a splendid gesture to send a Christmas card to Lev.

It took the rest of the evening for everyone to sign it. It was far more than a Christmas card; it was a sign of affection, an act of remembrance, a piece of diplomacy. Much time was spent by each individual on the entries which ranged in the final analysis from "I remember you at Molineux", to "Good luck Lev". There was even a "Best Wishes for the future." Names were signed below the messages.

By the end of the night there were ten inscriptions on the card. There was still a lot of space and not a few sentiments that old such and such would like to sign this, he always "guz on" about that match. Karl was entrusted to find where to send it. In the meantime other signatures would be sought.

3) The Setback

Of the original group, Karl was the youngest. One apart really. Not of their generation at all, but the next one with its Beatles and Rolling Stones instead of Frank Sinatra and Frankie Laine; with its England of Charlton, Moore and Banks instead of Lofthouse and Matthews. Karl felt at ease in his loose affiliation with older men. Only one of "Bill's cronies", which was Karl's collective term for them, seemed to mind the younger presence but the argument was one of allegiance rather than age. Karl never learnt the surname of this Jack whose jibes about the Albion always seemed to border on malice. His "football" was based on rivalry and apparently always had been. Karl wondered at times why Bill and the others put up with him.

The fact was that Jack was struck with Bill because he regarded Wolves as the greatest. That Bill always qualified that statement with a when and moreover, that he always stated why, was conveniently forgotten by Jack. For his part he could not see for the life of him why Karl was tolerated.

A few weeks after the idea to send Christmas greetings to Lev Yashin had been put into action the Wolves had a home game. In the evening the bar of *The Light* was full of young men who had been drinking since the end of the game. Wanderers had won and they were well watered. Jack had passed the time of day with most of them at one time or another and knew several quite well. Most of them were good supporters of their team; several, the ones Jack knew best, were trouble-makers more interested in the South Bank than the team they crowed about loudly.

Jack was well watered himself when Bill and the rest of them assembled. Karl noticed that the mood in the bar was quite ugly.

"It only wants a bus trip in for it to go over the top," he observed as he ordered. The gaffer assured him that there wasn't a trip in that night.

Karl was surprised to be prevented from continuing this conversation by Jack who loudly beckoned him to produce "that Christmas card" as he had some "supporters of football" who would sign it. Karl took out the card from his inside pocket and handed it to Jack. He thought nothing of handing the card over as he immediately engaged Bill in a conversation on the noise level. Jack got up and took the card to the bar with him. He didn't return to his seat however as he had signatures to collect.

"Here it is" he told the young men who broke momentarily from their revelry. "That card I told you about,... to that goalie."

One of them took it from him and focused on the signatures and inscriptions. It didn't make much sense and he would have thrust it back had it not been for Jack's insistence, "it's only for Wolves fans to sign... he came over to play at Molineux in the '50s."

Another young man who had a little less beer inside him asked which team this goalie played for. Jack told them it was Moscow Dynamo which was the equivalent of the Russian national team. The first young man put pen to paper and encouraged the others to do likewise as he now understood the object of the exercise. The task induced an even greater noise level in the band, who started chanting their terrace slogans.

The card was returned to Karl with messages to one of the greatest goalkeepers who ever lived such as "Wolves Rule Albion Bastards"; or "Wolves Rule Commie Bastards"; "You Reds Are Dead!"; "South Bank"; and "Lev Who?".

Karl looked at Bill in despair.

"We'll do another one." Bill entreated. "And that bloody yobbo won't get sight of it next time" he added, gesturing towards Jack.

4) Christmas Card To Lev

In a Moscow hospital Lev Yashin received his Christmas card from the football fans of Dudley. It was March by the time he got it. Karl had searched high and low for an address and ended up sending it to the Soviet embassy in London. Bill changed the inscription. It read:

We are football fans from Dudley in the English west midlands. It is a small industrial town but it produced one of the world's best footballers - Duncan Edwards. Most of the people follow the fortunes of Wolverhampton Wanderers or West Bromwich Albion. Many great sides and many great players have graced their pitches. You were one of the greatest. You will always live in the memories of those privileged to see you play.

Best wishes.

Lev Yashin opened the card. He could not read English but he had been to England many times. He recalled a cold November day in Wolverhampton.

FORTHCOMING PUBLICATION FROM THE KATES HILL PRESS

A WITNESS FOR PEACE

BY GREG STOKES

15th April 1986: In the early hours of the morning planes of the U.S.A. bombed targets in Libya - an act condemned across the globe. In the early afternoon Doug Stokes was murdered in Marrakesh by an Arab looking for Americans - an act reported across the globe as that of a "crazed knifeman running amok".

A Witness For Peace tells the real story.

It is a powerfully written account which takes the reader from a working class life which ended in tragic death, through a stoic fight with intransigent insurers and indifferent politicians, to an ultimate statement of hope for the future.

A Witness For Peace is a moving story which is at times angry and indignant, though not without flashes of humour. The work critically analyses the product of the media as well as describing their excesses in obtaining it; it tackles the issue of crime and insanity in a case where the culprit got away with it; and it examines the role of professionals in an expanding bereavement counselling industry. The conclusions are startling.

Publication date: April 1994.
Advance Orders: The Kates Hill Press
126 Watsons Green Road, Dudley.